SHOOT-OUT AMONG THIEVES

"I told you what would happen if you messed with the girl before we got the ransom," Lansdale said.

Holt answered, "I ain't gonna hurt her none, Tate. You just go on back to your sleepin' roll and let me handle this."

"I can't do that, Dwayne."

Katherine saw Lansdale's right hand slowly inch toward the Colt on his right hip.

"Forget it, Tate. You're an old man. You ain't fast enough to take me," Holt challenged, but Katherine sensed a hint of uncertainty in his voice.

"Only one way to find out, Dwayne."

"Tate, I got no want to—"

Holt did not finish his sentence. His right hand dropped, closing around the revolver's grip.

Lansdale moved at the same time. His Colt cleared its holster and spat lead before Holt could even free his weapon.

"Wha . . ." A surprised gasp quavered from Holt's lips. A heartbeat later, Holt collapsed. His body jerked spasmodically in its dance of death as he lay facedown in the sand.

The Stagecoach Series
Ask your bookseller for the books you have missed

STAGECOACH STATION 45:

PRESIDIO

Hank Mitchum

 Created by the producers of
Wagons West, The Badge,
Abilene, and **Faraday.**

Book Creations Inc., Canaan, NY · Lyle Kenyon Engel, Founder

BANTAM BOOKS

NEW YORK · TORONTO · LONDON · SYDNEY · AUCKLAND

PRESIDIO

*A Bantam Book / Published by arrangement with
Book Creations, Inc.*

Bantam edition / January 1990

*Produced by Book Creations, Inc.
Lyle Kenyon Engel, Founder*

ISBN 0-553-28309-X

Published simultaneously in the United States and Canada

*Bantam Books are published by Bantam Books, a division of
Bantam Doubleday Dell Publishing Group, Inc. Its trademark,
consisting of the words "Bantam Books" and the portrayal of a
rooster, is Registered in U.S. Patent and Trademark Office and
in other countries. Marca Registrada. Bantam Books, 666 Fifth
Avenue, New York, New York 10103.*

PRINTED IN THE UNITED STATES OF AMERICA

OPM   0 9 8 7 6 5 4 3 2 1

STAGECOACH STATION 45

PRESIDIO

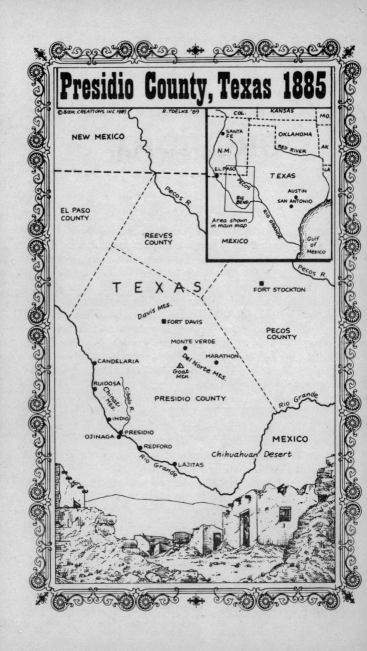

Presidio County, Texas 1885

© BOOK CREATIONS INC 1989   R. TOELKE '89

Chapter One

Thunder rolled through the Del Norte Mountains of West Texas. But this thunderous roar had just blasted from the barrel of a Colt .45, not from the green-tinged storm clouds that eerily blackened the afternoon sky overhead.

Tate Lansdale turned his back on the bay gelding that had dropped heavily to the muddy road, legs jerking spasmodically as life fled its body. Methodically Lansdale rotated the cylinder of the gun in his hand, ejected the spent shell, and then slipped in a fresh .45 caliber cartridge pulled from the gun belt around his waist. He double-checked the Colt's six chambers to reassure himself that the revolver carried a full load before sliding the weapon back into its holster.

Walking to a stand of thick-boled cottonwoods that stood to the side of the road, Lansdale approached a saddled chestnut hidden behind the ancient trees. From the mount's saddlebags he took a yellow slicker and slipped it over his head. He then pulled an empty flour sack from the saddlebag and stuffed it into a pocket.

The rain gear left him feeling encumbered and cramped. Worse, the Colt now lay beyond easy reach. If he needed it, he would have to fumble his way under the slicker to free the revolver from its holster. A man could die several times over in the time required to accomplish that simple task.

Yet, with the thunderstorms that had rolled up from Mexico and pushed across the Big Bend region of Texas for the past two days, it would appear suspicious for him not to be wearing a slicker. What he wanted today was sur-

1

prise, not suspicion. If the scheme he had in mind went off as planned, he would strike quickly and then fade into the mountains long before the sheriff in Monte Verde got wind of his deeds and formed a posse.

Besides, Lansdale told himself, if things came off as he planned this afternoon, there would be no need for the six-gun or the Winchester he eased now from the saddle boot and carefully checked to make certain it too was fully loaded. Still, he could not shake a niggling sensation of distrust in spite of the rifle's familiar weight in his hands.

He had always preferred a revolver to a rifle. Of the twenty men he had killed, he had used a rifle on only three of them. A rifle was better suited for dealing with rabbits and deer. With men one had to get up close before drawing a gun.

Assured the Winchester was loaded and ready, Lansdale moved back to the road. His gaze shifted to the dead-still bay sprawled across the muddy road. He sucked at his teeth in disgust. Killing the animal had been a waste of good horseflesh, but he had had to do it. The fact that the bay had not belonged to him eased his regret somewhat. Todd and Kelly had stolen the gelding from a small ranch north of Fort Stockton four days back. The two Carter brothers surely knew their business when it came to stealing horses. They had not left any tracks.

Reaching beneath the slicker, Lansdale tugged a watch from his pocket and thumbed it open—two o'clock. Only fifteen minutes until the Saturday stage rolled along this twisting road on its way from Marathon to Monte Verde.

Fifteen minutes. The phrase echoed in Lansdale's mind as his gaze lifted to the eroded, round granite boulders lining the narrow passage through the Del Nortes. Mottled with lichen and moss, both turned a velvet green from the rains, the boulders stood as high as two men and as wide as three. From his position in the middle of the road, Lansdale saw the flicking tail of Ray Powell's strawberry roan twenty feet to the left. But he saw no hint of Dwayne Holt or the Carter brothers, nor of the half-breed Billy Crow and Hank Yoakum, who had hidden themselves on opposite sides of the road. Nor would the stagecoach driver.

Fifteen minutes, Lansdale thought again. A mere quarter of an hour before he was on his way to becoming a rich man!

Taking the flour sack from the slicker, Lansdale pulled it over his head and adjusted the makeshift hood so that the crude holes cut into the cloth opened before his eyes. He then concealed the Winchester beneath the slicker's long, yellow skirt as he squatted in the mud beside the dead bay and waited.

Lightning lanced in glaring bolts from the green-black underbellies of swiftly moving storm clouds. Like jagged spider legs it danced over the rounded crests of the mountains. A stunted live oak halfway up the side of a grass-covered slope exploded in a shower of shattered bark and splintered wood as one of the blinding bolts attacked. Thunder, like the roar of a cannon, rolled through the West Texas mountains as sound caught up with the brilliant explosion of electric light. Yellow-red flames leapt from the oak's ragged stump despite the silver-dollar-sized raindrops that suddenly fell thickly from the sky.

"Oh!" Martha Morehead gave a little start, sitting straight on the stagecoach seat. Her eyes were saucer round and darted back and forth. "Lordy, that was too close for comfort!"

Katherine McQuay released the stage window's leather curtain, which she had held open with a slim finger so she could watch the storm's fireworks, and glanced at the middle-aged woman seated across the gently rocking coach from her. "There's nothing to be worried about, Mrs. Morehead. The lightning struck at least a mile away—high up on a mountain to our right."

The older woman smiled weakly at the only other female passenger among the six people in the coach. Pressing a hand to her bosom, she rolled her eyes to the men around her as though saying, "What has become of this younger generation?"

Katherine hid an amused smile behind a hand lifted to brush aside an imaginary stray strand of hair from her forehead. The matron was at least forty years older than her own eighteen years, but the woman acted like one of the twittering "young ladies" Katherine had met during her first year of finishing school in Austin. The mock display of feminine frailty was not attractive, even in someone her own age; she found it triply distasteful in a mature woman who should have known better.

Leaving Mrs. Morehead to the comforting of a shoe salesman and an El Paso banker who sat to her left and right, Katherine once again edged the curtain back with a finger and stared curiously outside. The heavy rain that had pelted the Del Norte Mountains only moments ago had transformed to a gentle shower. The falling raindrops beat a soothing rhythm on the stage's roof.

"You find it fascinating, don't you?" Clay Throckmorton whispered as he leaned toward Katherine. "The storm, I mean. I've been watching you since we left Marathon. You haven't been able to take your eyes off it for the past twenty miles."

She glanced at the handsome young man beside her, smiled, and nodded. "Ever since I was a little girl I've watched storms like these."

Clay's head tilted back, and he too looked out the crack she had opened with a finger. "It is quite spectacular. Not at all like the sheet lightning we often get in the piney woods. I don't believe I've ever seen a storm as untamed as this one."

"They're like this every summer in this part of the country. It's the hot air coming up off the desert hitting the cool air of the mountains. The rains here in the summer are a lot like the monsoons I've read about. During the rest of the year rain is scarce, but in the summer there are storms almost every afternoon."

Katherine studied the strong lines of Clay's face. There was no doubt in her mind that he was attractive. And he was charming. Of all the young men she had met during the last year in Austin, Clay Throckmorton was the only one she had allowed to call on her more than three times.

The only one of my friends Mother has invited home for a visit, she thought, as booming thunder drew her gaze back to the window.

But then, the fact that Clay's father was the popular

Senator Herschel Wilson Throckmorton might have something to do with the invitation, Katherine realized. Senator Throckmorton, it was rumored among those in the know around the state capitol in Austin, was being groomed for the governor's mansion come the next election. Having her only daughter married to the son of a governor would fit Caitlyn McQuay's personal vision of the McQuay family's appropriate place in the scheme of things.

Marrying a governor, or even better a president of the United States, would, of course, suit her mother more, Katherine thought. On the other hand, she could already hear her mother suggesting that Clay would be considered "quite a catch by any young lady."

Katherine admitted that to herself. Clay intended to complete his studies at the university next year and then to take his bar exams. After a year or two of law practice in Austin to establish himself, he planned to enter politics, following in his father's footsteps.

Or riding on his coattails.

Katherine immediately chided herself for the unkind thought. Clay was more than capable. His grades put him at the top of his class, and the more influential law firms in Austin were already wooing him to join them when he passed the bar.

Still, Katherine could not shake a feeling that there was a seed of truth in her earlier reflection. To be certain, she liked Clay—perhaps more than any other man she had ever met. But whether she loved him was something else altogether.

As much as she enjoyed Clay's company, the feel of his arms around her, and the sensations he awoke within her body when they kissed, a doubt always reared its ugly head at the back of her mind when she began to examine their relationship—a doubt as to what Clay's true intentions were.

The intentions she meant had nothing to do with the conduct of a man with a young woman. Clay always remained the perfect gentleman with her, whether they were in public or private. Even his stolen embraces and kisses were always within the boundaries of propriety. On more than one occasion Katherine had speculated pleasantly about what it would be like if Clay would allow social restraints to crumble for a moment and let passion rule.

The intentions she meant were those Clay had for her in his life.

It was not vanity, but rather honesty—and gratitude for her good fortune—that made Katherine realize how she, too, was considered a "good catch." She had been told by more than one man that she was beautiful, having inherited her mother's good looks largely in the deep auburn hue of her hair and the emerald of her eyes. At age forty-three Caitlyn McQuay still turned the head of every man she met, no matter what his age.

And there was the matter of the McQuay money. Following the Civil War, her father, J.D. McQuay, had come to the Big Bend region of Texas and had carved a ranching empire out of the wild land. Although Katherine had never heard any concrete figures on her family's wealth, she knew they were rich, even by Austin standards. Marrying into money had never hurt the career of a would-be politician.

"I've never been to this part of the state." Clay leaned back, his gaze returning to Katherine. "It's a lot different than I expected. I thought it would be all rock and sand, not these mountains and especially not the green prairie we've passed through today."

"Between October and May it can get awfully dry through most of Presidio County. But the rains always come with the summer," Katherine answered.

Clay's gaze shifted to the outside for an instant and then came dancing back to Katherine, lingering on her. She felt a flush of embarrassment at her devious thoughts. There was no guile in Clay's brown eyes, only admiration—even adoration. When had she first begun to see motives behind others' actions that were not there?

Katherine knew the answer without having to probe too deeply. It had been when her mother had sent her to Austin. Life in the state capital, with its never-ending balls, parties, and social events, was a far cry from simple, quiet Monte Verde and Presidio County. In Austin even a casual morning greeting seemed to contain some hidden meaning. Nothing in Austin was what it appeared to be.

I've been away from this country too long. Katherine stared at the granite-faced cliffs that hemmed the narrow road. A full year away from home was indeed too long. She had forgotten how truly beautiful this land of stark extremes was. Gently rolling prairies of blue-green grass abruptly disappeared into rugged peaks of red-brown granite that thrust up from the earth without warning. Where a foothold could be gained on the slopes grew junipers, which Texans called cedars, and small-needled piñon pines. At the base of the mountains flourished cottonwoods, live oaks, and an occasional elm.

She smiled, remembering that her father called this land "God's country." If this were indeed a heaven on earth, hell lay less than fifty miles to the south. There the Chihuahuan desert pushed out of Mexico and across the Rio Grande, that natural boundary between artificially defined countries. The rock and sand Clay had expected to find here near Monte Verde reigned over half of the Big Bend region. The fires of this piece of hell came not from an inferno raging within the bowels of the earth, but from an unforgiving sun that would kill man or beast who ventured into the desert without an understanding of its ways.

Clay leaned to her ear again. "A penny for your thoughts."

Katherine smiled. "I was just thinking how much I love this country."

She wanted to tell him that returning here had her heart racing at double time—that it would be pounding at thrice that rate by the time Monte Verde came into sight. But she could not put her feelings, her pride, into simple words. The sensations she felt were not spurred by the moment, but were deep-rooted in happy memories of the first seventeen years of her life in this wondrous country.

"Will we be able to see the McQuay ranch when the stagecoach leaves these mountains?" Clay asked.

Katherine shook her head. "The Circle Q begins—"

"Whoa!" The stage driver abruptly shouted outside. "Whoa, damn you!"

The coach lurched and rocked as the four-horse team immediately responded by slowing its pace. Inside the

stage the six passengers reached out and grabbed anything
their hands could find to help them stay in their seats.

"What's going on?" blustered the El Paso banker.

A cowboy who had climbed into the stage at Marathon and had promptly fallen asleep slid halfway to the
floor before his eyes blinked open. "We in Monte Verde?"

Anchoring herself with her left hand, Katherine used
her right to roll up the window's curtain and tie it off. She
poked her head outside and peered through the light mist
to the road ahead. A lone man with his back to the
approaching stagecoach squatted beside a bay horse sprawled
amid puddles and mud.

"Folks," the driver called to his passengers as he
brought the team to a walk, "seems we got a man with a
horse down up ahead. Shouldn't take long to give the
pilgrim a hand, and then we'll be on our way again."

Under the driver's straining arms, the horses came to
a halt. When the driver spoke again, it was to the unfortu-
nate rider. "Friend, from the looks of it, you could use a
hand."

Katherine watched the man in the yellow rain slicker
rise and turn. She caught her breath, barely stifling the
surprised gasp that tried to escape her throat. The man
wore a hood, and in his hands was a rifle—aimed directly
at the stagecoach driver.

"The hands I want to see up high are yours and this
dude's who's ridin' shotgun," the hooded figure said,
thrusting the rifle's muzzle at the two men sitting on the
driver's seat to emphasize his words.

Pulling her head back into the coach, Katherine
glanced at her fellow passengers. "It's a holdup. We're—"

The sound of approaching horses drowned the rest of
her words. Through the window she saw three riders
wearing the same flour-sack hoods as the highwayman who
had waited in the middle of the road. Although the
windows on the opposite side of the coach were still
closed, she could hear other riders on that side, and she
surmised that the coach was surrounded by outlaws.

"We don't want to hurt no one. And ain't nobody goin'
to get hurt as long as y'all do like I say," a voice came from

outside. "Start by gettin' all your passengers outside— pronto!"

"You heard him," the driver said as he swung to the ground and opened the coach door beside Katherine. "You all better do just like he says."

The driver then turned back to the hooded man in the slicker, who stepped behind a stand of cottonwoods and rode out on the back of a chestnut. "We ain't carryin' nothin' of value—no strongbox, no mail—just makin' a run with six passengers to Monte Verde."

"We ain't after no gold or mail." The chief gunman nudged his horse forward. Only his dark, sinister eyes were visible through the holes cut in the hood. He peered at the passengers, who lined themselves beside the stage-coach. "We just want to take a young lady for a li'l ride. This 'un right here."

Katherine stepped back when the robber pointed his rifle directly in her face. She heard his words, but they did not make sense. *Why would they want me?* she wondered.

"Bring that filly 'round here and get Miss McQuay mounted up," the man in the slicker called to the other side of the stagecoach. "Ain't no need wastin' more time than need be. The sooner these people get into Monte Verde, the better it will be for us."

"Be right—"

The explosive report of a rifle ripped the words from the air. Katherine's head jerked to the right. The stage's shotgun guard doubled over clutching his chest and then fell from the driver's board to the mud. The man did not move.

"What in hell?" The slicker-cloaked man yanked the chestnut's head around. "I said there weren't to be no shootin'!"

"The son of a bitch was goin' for his shotgun," a hooded man in a rain-soaked red shirt answered with no hint of regret in his voice. "What was I supposed to do—let him take a bead on you, Tate?"

"You stupid bastard!" Anger seethed in the leader's voice. "You didn't have to shoot. You could've hit him with your rifle barrel. You could've—"

"Katherine, run!"

Katherine blinked. She heard Clay shout, felt him shove her to the right, but did not comprehend his meaning—until it was too late.

The young man leapt forward, hurling himself head-on at the nearest mounted highwayman. Gallant and courageous his act might have been, but it was also stupid. He had covered half the distance to the rider when a rifle jerked and fired. Groaning, Clay dropped to the ground and writhed. Both his hands clutched his chest; blood spurted through his fingers.

Katherine took two steps toward Clay before the man in the yellow slicker spurred his chestnut between her and her fallen companion. Once again, the muzzle of his rifle jabbed in her face.

"Li'l lady, unless you want more of these folks to get hurt, you'd better get on that filly over yonder and come along with us, like I suggested in the first place." The gunman's tone left no doubt he was capable of shooting everyone on the stage if that was what it took to get her to comply.

Katherine glanced to the left to see another hooded gunman lead a bay around the stagecoach. When she hesitated, the man in the slicker cocked the hammer of his Winchester with a thumb and pointed the rifle at Mrs. Morehead. The older woman stumbled back against the stage, her face drained of color, her mouth twisted in horror.

"No!" Katherine shouted. "Don't shoot. I'll do what you want. I'll go with you."

"Good. I'm glad we came to an understandin' so quickly." While Katherine did as he commanded, the man reached inside the slicker and withdrew a yellow envelope that he handed to the stage driver. "Take that to Mrs. J.D. McQuay in Monte Verde. And you be damned sure she reads each and every single word that's wrote there. Then you tell Mrs. McQuay that if she don't do exactly—and I mean *exactly*—what's in that letter, we'll kill her daughter. If she blinks her eyes or in any way acts like she don't believe you, then you tell just what happened here today. Tell her killin'—be it a man or a woman or a sweet young thing like her daughter—don't come hard for none of us. Understand?"

"Understood." The driver nodded. He was sweating profusely.

Beneath his hood Tate Lansdale smiled as he turned to his men and signaled them to move out. When Kelly Carter, leading the McQuay girl's bay, rode past, Lansdale fell in behind as the band rode east and then cut south off the road into a narrow valley that wound between the mountains.

In spite of the exhilaration that had his heart pounding like a steam engine, Lansdale found himself fighting back the anger that boiled up and threatened to destroy the pleasure of the moment. He had not wanted any shooting today. Dwayne Holt had damned well known that. Yet he had gunned down the stage's shotgun rider without batting an eye.

Hot-blooded young bastard! Lansdale cursed to himself. Holt was too wild and dangerous to be trusted; he saw that now. He would have to keep a sharp eye on him. Lansdale was sure as hell not going to risk one man's ruining his chance to get his hands on enough money to make him rich for the rest of his life.

Chapter Two

Wrong—something was wrong!

The pulse inside Caitlyn McQuay's temples hammered. She sucked in a long, steady breath and told herself that she was overreacting like a mother hen whose chicks were leaving the nest. After all, Katherine was no baby chick; she was a young woman, fully eighteen years old. And Katherine had left the nest a year ago when she had traveled east to Austin to attend finishing school.

It's just that she's coming home, Caitlyn reassured herself, trying to ignore the clenched tightness of her gloved hands. A year can bring a lot of changes in a person, especially to one as young as her daughter. Caitlyn did not know what to expect. And that was what had her so nervous.

She lied to herself. There was something else, something she could not quite fathom—and a glance around her said that many of Monte Verde's three hundred citizens, who had turned out to welcome Katherine home, shared Caitlyn's apprehension. She could read it on their doubt-lined faces.

The approaching stagecoach did not rock across the lush green prairie in a gentle rhythm. It jerked and jolted erratically, swaying dangerously on its overtaxed springs behind the four-horse team. The driver was whipping the animals like a madman. This close to town, he should be easing back on the reins, preparing to draw the horses to a halt.

Caitlyn's emerald eyes shifted to the man standing to her right. Although only five years older than her own forty-three, Els Brewster looked a decade older. The sheriff of Presidio County pulled a sweat-stained gray hat from his head and ran a hand over a scalp that was more skin than hair. As he tugged the wide-brimmed hat back on, his brown eyes darted to Caitlyn and then back to the stagecoach.

"What is it, Els?" Caitlyn's voice quavered. "Can you see something I can't?"

Els shrugged, his head wagging from side to side. "Don't see nothin'. The driver's just pushin' his team a li'l hard, that's all, Caitlyn. Nothin' to get yourself worked up over."

"Nothing to get myself worked up over! *My daughter* is on that stage! Els, if you were worth the—" Caitlyn caught herself before she unleashed a verbal tirade designed to cut Els to the quick. The lawman, whom she had known most of her adult life and considered a close friend, deserved better from her.

She forced her balled fist open and slowly drew in another deep breath. The instant she exhaled, her hands clenched again, and her heartbeat doubled its runaway pounding. The stagecoach did not slow down. "Something is wrong, Els. I can feel it. That driver is still using the whip on those horses."

"Caitlyn, you're—" The sheriff's words faded as though he had no answer for the handsome woman at his side. Nor did his eyes turn to her. His shoulders slumped wearily, helplessly.

"Pa, what's Clint Bomar up to?" Harlan Brewster wove his way through the crowd gathered on Monte Verde's main street. "He's going to kill that team or wreck the coach if he isn't careful."

Caitlyn glanced at the twenty-one-year-old man. Standing close to six feet tall, Harlan looked as young as his father looked old. The shiny deputy's badge pinned to the handsome young man's vest did nothing to give him the aura of maturity. Or was it her own mounting years that made him seem so young? She did not like to consider that. Els had been only a few years older than his son was now when she and J.D. had first met him. Now look at the difference—

"Robbers!" Alarm filled the voice that rose over the rattle and clank of the stage. "Murderers!"

"Oh, God!" Caitlyn's head jerked around. Strands of rich auburn hair fell askew from beneath the small green hat she wore.

"Robbers—seven of 'em!" The driver stood, using the weight of his whole body to pull back on the reins as the stagecoach rolled into town. "They hit us back in the Del Nortes! Killed Tom House and one of the passengers! Made off with—"

The sound of hooves, the clank of harnesses, and the buzz of the crowd coming alive drowned the driver's words. With the rest of Monte Verde's citizenry, Caitlyn surged anxiously toward the halted coach.

One of the stage's doors flew open and an overweight man in a black suit stepped out. "This young man isn't dead, but he's hurt awful bad. They shot him in the chest when he tried to help the girl."

Girl? A steel band constricted about Caitlyn's chest. Although her heart knew the answer, the question came from her lips, "What girl?"

She received no answer. A plump woman in a blue dress, tears streaming down her cheeks and her high-pitched voice wailing, staggered from the stagecoach. "Lord God Almighty! It was horrible. I thought they intended to kill me—or worse. We're lucky to be alive—all of us. They just came down on us. . . ."

Two men in the crowd grabbed the woman's arms as she stumbled, catching her before she fainted.

"What girl?" Caitlyn repeated loudly.

And still the question went unanswered as two other men, one in a brown suit and a derby, the other a cowboy, came out of the coach carrying the limp body of a man between them. A moist flower of crimson spread across the latter's chest.

"We done what we could to stop the bleedin', but he's in mighty poor shape." This from the cowboy. "Heard him say his name was Thack Morton or somethin' like that."

"Throckmorton." Caitlyn wanted to gasp out in horror—to break down and cry as panic sought to rob her of reason.

Instead she summoned every ounce of strength within her and pushed through the crowd. J.D. had taught her that—deal with the situation at hand, see it through, then handle what is inside when there is proper time to sort through the emotions that can rend a soul. "His name's Throckmorton—Clay Throckmorton, son of Senator Herschel Throckmorton. He was traveling with my daughter and was to be my guest at the Circle Q."

Every head turned to her, but no one moved, as though the citizens of Monte Verde were uncertain what to do.

"Els, have the young man taken right away to Dr. Callaway's before he bleeds to death." Caitlyn's authoritative voice betrayed none of the dread that filled her breast.

While the sheriff ordered four townsmen to do as Caitlyn said, she moved to the stage and looked inside. The coach was empty. Closing her eyes, she steadied herself with another deep breath before turning to the driver, who helped three other townsmen lower the body of the slain shotgun guard from the stage. "My daughter was on this stagecoach. Where is she?"

"Ma'am, them outlaws made off with her," the still nameless cowboy answered. "It was her they was after. They didn't even take the money off a none of us. They just took her and rode off."

"That's right. They weren't after nothin' but the young lady," the driver confirmed. "Fact is, that's exactly what they said—that they didn't want no gold or mail, just the girl."

"My daughter?" Caitlyn blinked; terror, like an icy spike, skewered deep to her heart. "They wanted my Katherine?"

Els stepped to Caitlyn's side. "You certain of that, Clint? They held up the stage just to take Miss Katherine?"

The driver nodded. "The shootin' didn't start till Tom went for his shotgun and that young feller tried to take on one of the gunmen. Damned fool thing that—that Throckmorton wasn't even totin' a hogleg. Never seen anythin' like him tellin' the girl to make a run for it while he went after one of the holdup men. The nasty dude was still high in the saddle. Must've been chewin' loco weed or somethin'. He never had a chance."

"My Katherine," Caitlyn repeated, the shock of the revelation leaving her dazed. "Why? Why would anyone do this?"

Harlan Brewster walked to his father's side. "Because she's Katherine McQuay. It's not like the McQuay name isn't known throughout most of Texas, Mrs. McQuay."

Caitlyn's gaze shot to Harlan. She flinched as his words drove home the cold truth of the words. He was right, and she knew it.

"Mrs. McQuay?" The stage driver's eyes widened. "Mrs. J.D. McQuay? Are you Mrs. J.D. McQuay?"

Caitlyn nodded. "I'm Caitlyn McQuay." She had not publicly acknowledged her husband's name for five years.

"One of them gave me this to pass on to you." The driver reached into a pocket and withdrew a folded yellow envelope that he handed over to Caitlyn. "He said I was to make sure that you read every word of it."

Tearing open the envelope, Caitlyn slipped out the single sheet of yellow paper folded within. The page was spotted with blotches of ink and the handwriting was little more than scratched-out printing, but the meaning was oh too plain. She felt the color drain from her cheeks as she read the short and simple message:

> If you want to see yur dawter alive agin bring half a millyun dollars to Presidio on the bordur two weeks from today. We will get word to you there as to wat to do next. This is no jok. We are desparat men and will kill the girl unless you do wat we say. Do not tell the law.

"Oh, God." Caitlyn closed her eyes. A cold shiver crawled up her spine. Speaking hoarsely to no one and everyone, she declared, "Katherine's been kidnapped. They're threatening to kill her unless I do what they want."

The driver nodded. "They said I was to tell you to look at Tom and that young feller to make sure that you understood they meant business."

"Let me see that." Els tugged the ransom note from her shaking fingers and quickly scanned it. "You ain't even considerin' doin' like they ask, are you, Caitlyn?"

Caitlyn swallowed back her fear. "I'll do whatever is

necessary to get my daughter back alive, Els—*whatever* is necessary."

The sheriff spat to the side. "There won't be any need of payin' anyone half a million dollars to get Katherine back—"

A hushed gasp ran through the crowd gathered around the stagecoach at the mention of the ransom price.

"I'll have Katherine back here in Monte Verde 'fore the day's out—tomorrow at the latest. Whoever these men are, they can't have gotten far," Els said. "All I got to do is get a posse up. I'll—"

"Els," Caitlyn cut him short, "I don't want anything done that will endanger my daughter. The note says not to involve the authorities."

Els's brown eyes met hers directly. "The authorities are *already* involved. Ain't no lowlifes goin' to get away with somethin' like this, not in Presidio County while I'm the sheriff. And not to a girl I think of as practically my own daughter."

He turned from Caitlyn and called to the men around him. "I need twenty men who can be armed with pistol and rifle and be ready to ride in ten minutes."

"Els," Caitlyn attempted to stop him.

It was too late. Not just twenty, but half the men gathered shouted out their intention to ride after the gunmen who had so boldly kidnapped the daughter of Caitlyn McQuay.

"Caitlyn, you let ol' Moss drive you back to the Circle Q in your surrey, and you wait for us there. I'll bring Katherine back to you. I promise you that."

"Els," Caitlyn started again.

The sheriff would not hear her. He pivoted and trotted toward his office with Harlan close at his heels. Thirty men scattered up and down the main street to untether their horses and check their rifles.

Caitlyn cursed under her breath. This was all wrong; she could feel it. These men were not part of a posse anyone could count on, but performers in some circus. It was as though they were off to hunt some rogue cougar that had come down out of the mountain to prey on stray

steers. Theirs was not the sober attitude of men intent on
rescuing a kidnapped young woman.

The worst of them was Els Brewster himself. She saw
that reflected in his blazing eyes and in the blind determi-
nation of his voice. Once Caitlyn would have trusted Els
to make good his promise. But that had been in younger
days for both of them.

The years weighed heavily on Els; he had grown too
slow and cautious for the badge he had worn for two
decades. During the past year rumors had flown thick and
heavy that when the next election came around Presidio
County would find itself another man to wear that badge.
For Els this new mission was not just about rescuing
Katherine, but about proving to himself and the county
that he was still worthy of the office he held.

The problem was, Caitlyn knew, as surely as Els must
have recognized in his own heart, he was no longer up to
the task. Nor was his son ready for the job: Harlan had all
the makings of a good man, but as yet he lacked the
experience to stand in his father's boots.

No, there was only one man whom she could trust to
return her daughter to her safe and sound or give his own
life trying. That man was in some godforsaken, dusty town
in the New Mexico Territory called Las Cruces.

"Boys, I intend to ride hard and long. If you ain't up
to stickin' with me, now's the time to pull out." With that
Els mounted and spurred a bay toward the east. Behind
him rode a disorganized army of forty men.

For a long, silent moment, Caitlyn watched the posse
depart. Then she turned and with steady strides walked
toward Monte Verde's telegraph office. There was a possibility that Els might prove true to his word, but she would
not risk Katherine's life on that. She knew she had several
telegrams to send if she were going to raise the half
million demanded by the gunmen in a hurry. But most
important was the one telegram she intended to wire to
Las Cruces.

Chapter Three

Tate Lansdale reached for a pouch of tobacco in his shirt pocket and then jerked his hand away. A self-satisfied smile slid across his scruffy face as he pulled a plug of chewing tobacco from the back pocket of his breeches and bit off a chew.

Mother Lansdale didn't raise no fool. His smile broadened as he sat cross-legged on a flat-topped boulder and casually spat a dark stream of spittle to one side. He wanted a smoke, but a chew would have to do for now. He had given orders that there would be no fires, not even a match, while they were camped in the mountains. The red glow of a burning cigarette was enough to give a man away, especially at night or at dusk like it was now.

And if there was one thing he was certain of, there would be men out looking for him and his boys after what they had pulled off that afternoon. His note might have told Mrs. J.D. McQuay to stay clear of the law, but he did not expect her to do so. He knew a posse would be scouring the hills for them.

He had planned for a posse! All day yesterday, he and the boys had laid down so many false trails that even a pure-blooded Comanche Indian would get himself lost trying to follow all of them. And there had not been any Comanches to speak of in Texas for over ten years.

Spitting to the side again, Lansdale looked out over the terrain below. Nothing, he saw nothing but seven mule deer grazing at the base of the mountain on which he sat. Maybe the false trails had been better than he reckoned. He chuckled to himself. He would have given

odds that by now he would have sighted a posse out of
Monte Verde.

No, Lansdale gave himself another mental pat on the
back, *my mother didn't raise no fool.*

In the twenty-one years that had passed since he had
stolen his pa's old pistol and run away from home at age
fifteen, Tate Lansdale had given little thought to his
mother. Yet, in the past couple of weeks, she had popped
into his head time and again. For the first time in his life
Lansdale was grateful to the Bible-thumping, hickory-
switch-wielding old battle-ax. Until now he had never
seen any use for the seven years of schooling she had
forced on him—the seat of his breeches warmed to glow-
ing by that hickory switch each morning as a sharp reminder for him to behave in class.

The fact was he had found no need of reading or
writing in his chosen professions, whatever they might be
from one week to the next. Rustler, horse thief, highwayman, bank robber, or hired gun had little use for the
printed word, unless it was to double-check the names on
wanted posters, which to date had never carried the name
of Tate Lansdale. Ranging his activities from Missouri to
California had helped to see to that. If there was a single
rule Lansdale lived by, it was to never stay put for very
long in one place or something or someone might catch up
with you.

Even then a man had to be careful—damned careful.
Thirty-six years for a man who chose to walk the path he
walked was tantamount to old age. Those who made their
livelihood by the gun were lucky to see thirty years. It was
a matter of odds. The longer a man lived, the more
chances he had of making a mistake that would get him
too intimately acquainted with a bullet or put him on the
wrong end of a rope.

Lansdale had thought he had met that bullet nine
months ago in Kansas. The range war had been small and
had not even attracted the notice of the newspapers. But
the two clod busters who had bushwhacked him from
behind a poplar tree, put a slug of lead in his back, and
left him for dead had been all Lansdale needed to realize
that the odds were swinging against him.

He had managed to find his horse that night, re-
mount, and ride all the way into Abilene to a doctor who
dug the lead out of his back. After a month recovering in a
cheap rented room, he rode south. He had known it was
time for a change in his life, but exactly how or when that
change would come he had not been sure.

That is, until he read a newspaper article in Austin
about a Katherine McQuay, daughter of wealthy cattleman
J.D. McQuay, who was returning home for the summer
after her first year of finishing school. Katherine McQuay,
it seemed, had helped out on a charity ball. Just the kind
of thing those rich young kids loved to do, he thought
sarcastically. What Lansdale found interesting was the
mention that J.D. McQuay, who had a reputation as a
hard-nosed, no-nonsense son of a bitch among those Lansdale
rode with, no longer resided in Texas. Although the article
made no mention of where McQuay presently lived, it did
say that it was his wife who now ran the McQuays' huge
Circle Q Ranch and other extensive business interests.

It had not taken Lansdale more than three hours and
double that number of beers in an Austin saloon to put
one and one together and come up with a plan to separate
Mrs. J.D. McQuay from a sizable portion of the family
fortune. Now, with the kidnapping accomplished, all that
stood between him and a life of luxury in Mexico or maybe
all the way down in South America was two weeks and a
stretch of land between the Del Norte Mountains and the
town of Presidio, which sat on the Rio Grande to the
south.

Rio Bravo, Lansdale corrected himself. That's what
one called the Rio Grande if he lived south of it. And a
man could do a lot of living—enough to last him to a ripe
old age—with bona fide U.S. dollars to spend south of the
border. Tate was no banker or businessman. Quitting
school so early on had not left him with much firepower
for fancy arithmetic, either. But he had a knack for cleverness
in the way he lived outside the law, and he had definitely
learned more than a thing or two about how the world of
big money works.

Out on the range around the campfires at night, and
in the smoky barrooms of dusty cowpoke towns, Tate had

often heard stories told by his outlaw cronies about how far U.S. currency would stretch if you just took it across the river to spend in Mexico. Most fellows said they picked up twenty-five cents or more for every dollar they took into Mexican territory. In Tate's mind, these were stories about easy money—real easy.

But even more amazing were the tales told about the magical power of the Yankee dollar down in South America, in a place called Brazil. Tate would have been hard-pressed to locate Brazil on a map, but if it was true, as his buddies said it was, that one American dollar could put a whole two dollars' worth of Brazilian money in your pocket, then that was definitely the place for a Texas outlaw to go for a happy retirement.

Luxury and ease, Tate thought to himself. *Easy living for the rest of my days. That's what starts in just two weeks, when I carry that U.S. money across the Rio Grande and start getting richer and richer by the minute— just 'cause I'm smart and just 'cause it's all mine.*

Tate was convinced that a neat and tidy five hundred thousand dollars off the backs of the McQuays would turn him into a millionaire practically overnight. It was sweet to contemplate, mighty sweet. Worth the trouble and the risk—he had no doubts. A seven-way cut of the half million never crossed Lansdale's mind; divvying up the ransom was not part of his plans—although those riding with him would not know this key fact until it was too late. Lansdale's smile grew. The more he thought about South America, the more he liked the idea.

As Lansdale spat another dark stream of spittle and tobacco juice to the side, a movement below caught his eye. Dropping to his stomach, he inched to the edge of the boulder and peered at the narrow pass at the foot of the mountain. His heart thudded like a blacksmith's hammer on an anvil. This was it—the real test of the false trails he and the boys had laid yesterday.

There was no doubt in his mind that the riders below were a posse. Forty, maybe as many as fifty men—the distance and mounting darkness made it difficult to take an accurate count—did not ride together in this country unless they were a posse, or an army.

Lansdale held his breath as the men rode by without hesitating or even glancing up to his position. The smile returned to his face when the posse followed the cramped pass southward, sticking to the misleading trail he had cleverly placed there. That trail would take them ten miles farther south to a rain-swollen creek. The coming night would catch them before that. Which meant they would have to camp for the night and would not find the creek until tomorrow morning.

If things went as he planned, the posse would follow the creek in the belief that he and his men had taken to it to hide their trail. It would take another ten or twenty miles for the men to discover the ruse. By then the heat of the moment would have cooled. Half the men in the posse would no doubt find their taste for justice dulled and want to head back to Monte Verde. It would take another day or two for the rest of the men to realize there was no hope of sorting the real trail from the false ones.

And that will be the end of the posse! Lansdale grinned, pleased with himself and his prospects for the future. He and the boys would stick to his timetable. They would wait here tucked away in the Del Norte Mountains with their precious hostage for five days. Then they would ride south to Presidio and wait for Mrs. J.D. McQuay and the five hundred thousand dollars to arrive.

And should the posse somehow find its way through the false trails, Lansdale still had an ace up his sleeve. On the pack mule back in camp was a little surprise he had waiting to greet any fools who ventured too near the mountain.

"Tate?"

A whisper drew Lansdale from his woolgathering. He glanced behind him to see Billy Crow slip between two boulders. "Over here, Billy. What d'ya want?"

The half-breed glanced from left to right before locating Lansdale. "You told me to spell you when it started to get dark."

"Right." Lansdale pushed to his feet and then dropped to the ground to let Billy take his position. "If you see anythin'—*anythin*'—I want to know about it. Understand?"

"Understood." Billy nodded and then folded his legs

under his body and slowly sank atop the boulder. Without another word he stared below, never glancing back as Lansdale moved along the narrow deer path that wove among the jumble of granite boulders.

Lansdale shook his head. Billy had too much Indian blood in his veins to suit him. Indians always acted so damned strange, like they saw things a white man's eyes could not see. It sent chills up and down Lansdale's spine.

Still, without Billy he would never have found this camp. Billy claimed to be Lipan Apache, born to a white captive and the war chief Red Shirt. For all Lansdale knew, Billy might be telling the truth. He sure knew these mountains, and he was old enough to have lived in them before the Lipans were driven out of Texas before the Civil War.

The path widened to a granite-floored clearing a hundred feet long and thirty wide near the crest of the mountain. There was more than enough sheltered space here for the horses and Lansdale's men. A weathered crack in the mountain's face ran back about ten feet in the solid rock to form a cave just large enough to permit them to take cover when the summer rains came. In front of the mouth of this narrow cave his men had spread their sleeping rolls.

"Heard horses a few minutes back." Hank Yoakum looked up from the twist of jerked beef he was gnawing on. "The posse?"

"They never slowed down as they headed south." Lansdale nodded.

Chuckles of approval rose from the Carter brothers' throats. "Damn smart thinkin', those false trails, Tate." Kelly grinned up. "They'll be halfway to the desert 'fore they realize what we pulled."

Lansdale did not return the grin. Dwayne Holt was nowhere to be seen, nor was Katherine McQuay. "Where's the girl—and where the hell's Dwayne?"

Ray Powell stretched out his lanky body atop his blankets and jabbed a thumb to the left. "The girl had private business to attend. Dwayne took her over yonder to that cedar brake. Said he'd stick close and make sure it was only her business she was a mind to do."

This also brought a chuckle from the Carter brothers. Their amusement died as a rattle in their throats when Lansdale shot them a disapproving glance. "How long have they been gone?"

"'Bout fifteen minutes," Powell answered.

"You stupid bastards!" A cold chill crawled up Lansdale's spine. Holt was the last of the men he wanted alone with the girl!

Pivoting, he hastened across the clearing to a deer path leading to a cluster of bushy, stunted junipers that was more a copse than a full brake. The muffled cries of distress coming from within the bushes told him his instincts were right. He crashed through the prickly branches.

At the center of the cedars was a patch of sand no more than six feet by three. Holt was on top of the girl there. His left hand was clamped firmly over her mouth while his right hand alternately fended off her blows and tore at the buttons on the bodice of her dress.

Lansdale's right hand dropped to the holstered Colt on his right hip. With a slight flick of the wrist he brought the revolver up and thumbed back the hammer. The muzzle of the weapon swung directly to the center of Holt's back. "Get off of her, Dwayne! And I mean now, if you ever want to see the sun rise on a new day."

An ugly sound that passed for a laugh rumbled in Holt's throat. He slowly rolled from the girl, who scurried away on her hands and knees, and grinned slyly up at Lansdale. "You ain't gonna go and shoot me, Tate. You and I both know that—not with that posse so close. A gunshot would bring 'em down on top of us in a matter of minutes."

Lansdale cursed to himself. His forefinger, which had begun to squeeze down on the trigger, hesitated. As much as he wanted to finish what he had started and eliminate the young gunman before he caused more trouble, Holt was right. A gunshot would echo off these mountains for miles around and alert the posse.

That moment's hesitation was all the opening Holt needed. With the speed of a striking snake, he pushed to his feet and leapt forward, arms extended wide to encircle Lansdale and drag him to the ground.

Had Lansdale blinked at the unexpected attack, Holt would have brought him down and been on top of him in a split second. Lansdale did not blink. Instead he sidestepped, evading those ensnaring arms by a hairsbreadth. At the same time he swiped out with the Colt. The barrel slammed solidly into the side of Holt's head.

With a yelp of pain the man dropped to the sand, rolling there as he clutched both hands to the side of his face.

"Don't ever pull somethin' stupid like that again." Lansdale lowered the Colt's muzzle, pointing it directly at Holt's nose. "You so much as touch her again, and I'll kill you. I swear I'll cut you down like a rabid dog. Until we have the money, I don't even want a hair on her head out of place."

"You won't get no more trouble out of me, Tate. Now that I know the way it is." Holt nodded his acquiescence as he staggered to his feet. "You're the head honcho on this job and what you say goes."

The words were right; Holt's voice carried the correct tone of submission. However, the cold glint of his dark eyes told Lansdale the words and tone were all for show. Sooner or later Holt and he would face each other again to settle what they had begun this evening.

Holt turned and took three unsteady steps toward the camp; then he halted and leered back at Katherine. "And after we get that money, sweetheart, then you're mine."

Again Lansdale's finger tightened around the trigger. For a second time he caught himself just before he squeezed down; the posse was still too near to risk a gunshot. As hard as it was for him to do, he slipped the Colt back into its holster as Holt moved off through the cedars.

Lansdale swung around to face Katherine. For several moments he stared at the girl. She was a bit young for his taste, but it was hard for him to remember ever seeing a woman so pretty. It was not difficult to understand why Holt had gotten worked up like a bull in rut. "Get up from there. You've caused enough trouble for one day."

When the girl did not respond to his command, he reached down, grabbed one of her arms and wrenched her to her feet. "I got some spare duds back in my saddlebag.

We'd better get you out of that dress so you won't look so much like a woman."

He pushed her toward the camp. The two weeks before the meeting in Presidio were going to be longer than he had anticipated. His only hope was that the rest of the boys would not start getting any ideas into their heads. Holt was a big enough problem as it was.

Chapter Four

"I want to keep him here two or three more days just to make doubly certain my prognosis is correct." Dr. Weldon Callaway opened the door to his cool and dark home and allowed Caitlyn McQuay to step out into Monte Verde's bright sunlight again.

"But you're sure he'll be all right?" Although the physician had told her five times that Clay Throckmorton was well on his way to recovery from his gunshot wound, she still found it hard to believe. The young man had been barely alive when the men had lowered him gingerly from the stagecoach three days ago.

"He's young and he's strong. Give me a few more days to keep an eye out for infection, and then I'll place him in your able hands. Nothing in the world will get him back on his feet quicker than the good, red McQuay beef you serve out at the Big House," the doctor assured her for the sixth time.

Caitlyn hid her automatic wince behind a quick smile when she heard the term "Big House." J.D. had rudely dubbed the home he had built for her—under no small amount of protest—the "Big House," saying it went beyond the needs of a rancher and smacked too much of the ostentatious mansions in Houston, Austin, or Jefferson. That the name had stuck years after J.D. had gone his own way was a constant reminder of a life Caitlyn had tried to place behind her.

She could well imagine the gleam of amusement in J.D.'s eyes should he learn of her irritation. And the name was irritating; it sounded as though she resided in a prison. The opulence of the Circle Q's main house was anything but the dank gloom of a penitentiary. She had personally seen to that. The most notable personages of Texas society were frequent guests at the ranch. The soirees she held were envied by other socialites throughout the state and were regularly gossiped about in all the major society columns.

"I'll send a rider out to the Circle Q in a few days when I feel that Mr. Throckmorton is well enough to be moved," Callaway said.

"Then I'll have a guest room prepared for him." Caitlyn nodded and started to walk away; then she paused and looked back at the venerable physician. "And, Weldon, thank you for all you've done."

The doctor smiled wryly. "You might want to withdraw that thank-you when you get my bill."

Caitlyn returned his smile and walked down Monte Verde's main street toward the stage office, where her surrey and Moss, her driver, waited. From a small, beaded wrist satchel she took a gold watch and thumbed it open. The timepiece appeared large and bulky in her dainty, white-gloved hands. It was a man's pocket watch and had belonged to her great-grandfather. Once she had hoped to present the timepiece to James and then Timothy on their eighteenth birthdays. But the Lord in his unfathomable wisdom had called both frail infants back to his bosom before either had seen more than a month of life on this earth. Now she held this most cherished possession in trust for the son she hoped Katherine would one day soon bring into this world.

Katherine. The horror, the fear, the sheer terror Caitlyn had managed to keep contained within her the last three days surged upward and threatened to overwhelm her. She stumbled, the world spinning. Since J.D. had left years ago without so much as packing his bags, their daughter had become her world. Now she had no guarantee Katherine was even still alive. All she could do was pray that—

Caitlyn shook her head to dispel the fear. *No.* She drew in three deep breaths and slowly exhaled them. There was nothing to be gained from such negative thoughts.

If all her years with J.D. had taught her anything, it was to face the cards life dealt and play them out. Katherine *was* alive. She had to continue hanging on to that hope. She could not believe differently.

Drawing herself up straight, she once more glanced at the pocket watch, snapped it shut, returned it to her satchel, and continued toward the stagecoach office. It was noon exactly. If the special stage she had ordered from El Paso were running on time, it would arrive in Monte Verde within the next half hour. Then she could place Katherine's fate in the ablest pair of hands she knew.

As she reached the comforting shade of an awning that ran along the front of the office, she turned and studied the small town. Nothing appeared changed in Monte Verde. Her daughter had been kidnapped and was being held for half a million dollars in ransom, but the town's life rolled on as though nothing had happened.

Her gaze shifted to the sheriff's office. She choked back a wave of disgust. Els Brewster and the last ten members of his posse had returned to town this morning, hangdog and empty-handed. Els had not had the courage to face her and say that he had failed—that he had been unable to find even a trace of the seven men who had abducted her daughter. Like a whipped mutt with his tail tucked between his legs, he had slunk into his office and hidden there. She had expected no better from Els, but to be proven right only intensified her disgust.

"The stage, Mrs. McQuay." Moss stood in the surrey and jabbed an arm to the west. "She's a-comin' in now."

Caitlyn's gaze followed his pointing finger across the miles of rolling prairie that stretched between Monte Verde and the Davis Mountains thirty miles to the west. With only one passenger and no cargo to weigh her down, the stage seemed to fly over the grasslands. Apparently the driver had fully understood his instructions that he was to make the long haul from the Texas-New Mexico border without undue delay.

Ten minutes passed before the stagecoach rolled into town with the six-horse team lathered in sweat. The driver shouted at the animals and hauled back on the reins. The coach halted directly in front of the office.

"He's inside, Mrs. McQuay." The driver threw on the brake and wiped his brow with a shirt sleeve. "He came just like you said he would."

Caitlyn's thinly plucked right eyebrow arched high as she looked from driver to coach door. The stage's curtains were fully raised, and no one sat inside.

The stage driver leapt to the ground. Befuddlement clouded his face when his own gaze surveyed the empty coach. "I don't understand." He reached out, tugged a brass handle down, and pulled open the door.

A dog, a large dog, a very large dog, leisurely picked itself up from the stage's wooden floor, climbed to its four fist-sized feet, and stood staring at Caitlyn out of one wild robin's-egg-blue eye and one brown eye, while its tongue hung out thirstily from the side of its mouth. The creature was the ugliest animal to claim canine ancestry that Caitlyn had ever beheld. With a coat that erratically changed colors from brown to white to speckled gray, the long-haired dog appeared to be part German shepherd, part collie, and part alley mongrel.

"I don't understand, ma'am." The driver's bewilderment grew the longer he stared at the dog. "He was inside with this mutt when I pulled out of the last way station. I swear he was."

"Apparently *he* didn't approve of the travel accommodations I arranged for him." Caitlyn made no attempt to conceal her disgust for both the situation and the mongrel still staring at her, its tail wagging back and forth in friendly fashion and its tri-toned ears pricked forward alertly.

With a snort of disapproval, Caitlyn turned her back on the stage and climbed into the waiting surrey. Only then did she look back at the mongrel that watched her every move. "Oh, all right. Come on, General Lee, if you must."

A happy sound that was a cross between a bark and a yelp escaped the dog's mouth. In one bound it exited the stage and covered half the distance to the surrey. Two quick strides and it leapt into the seat beside Caitlyn, nuzzling its head against her hand to have its ears scratched. She obliged the animal.

"'Cuse me, ma'am, but I got the feelin' that you never laid eyes on that dog till I opened the coach." The driver pulled off his hat and scratched his head.

"I hadn't," Caitlyn assured him.

"Then how come you knowed the mutt's name?"

"*He* isn't the most creative man I've ever met." Caitlyn heaved a sigh in spite of herself. "Every dog *he* has ever owned he's named General Robert E. Lee." She waved a hand to Moss. "It's time to take the General and me home."

The surrey driver clucked forward the matched pair of chestnut mares harnessed to the rig and eased them southward, leaving a totally perplexed stagecoach driver standing beside an empty stage.

Caitlyn glanced at the dog that stared at her with obvious affection and demanded its ears be scratched some more. The mongrel certainly held some meaning. She knew that. But she could not fathom what her estranged husband had in mind.

J.D. McQuay speared the last bite of steak with a fork, popped it in his mouth, and used half a biscuit to slop the gravy left pooled on the plate before depositing that in his mouth. He leaned back in his chair, heaved a satisfied sigh, and patted a stomach filled with steak, fried potatoes, biscuits, butter, and honey. "That was one fine meal, Mrs. Simmons."

A young woman, no more than twenty-four years old, turned from the dishes she was washing and smiled at J.D. "The way you enjoy your food, Mr. McQuay, you'd make any woman feel like she was the best cook in the world. You ate that steak like a man who hadn't seen a hot meal in a month of Sundays. Care for another cup of coffee?"

"It seems like a year since I last ate, but in truth I haven't had a decent meal since leaving Las Cruces nearly three days ago." He held up his cup and let her fill it. In some ways the young rancher's wife reminded him of Caitlyn when they had first married, at least in height and the distinctive color of her hair. Mary Simmons was attractive enough, but Caitlyn had been beautiful—had still been beautiful when he had seen her five years ago.

"Excuse me, Mr. McQuay, but you're a lot younger man than I expected. From all I've heard about J.D. McQuay and the things you've done, I expected you to be older than Methuselah himself. You're quite a legend in these parts."

"Thank you, ma'am. I'd hate to think I looked as old as I feel." J.D. lifted his coffee cup in a salute to the woman.

As nice as Mrs. Simmons's compliment was, he did not take it seriously. J.D. McQuay knew that he looked every bit of his forty-five years, and then maybe a few years more; he saw his all-too-familiar reflection in a mirror each morning when he shaved.

Although he still had every strand of hair that had been on his head twenty-five years ago, somehow, effortlessly, about a fourth of the dark brown mass had transformed itself to threads of silver. The rock-hard stomach he had once boasted now rounded out to a slight paunch. A few years back he had quietly admitted to himself that he had passed the prime of life without really noticing it. He had reached that time in life where six feet and two hundred pounds might still be physically imposing, but he knew that from here on out there would be far fewer aches and pains to endure if a man could use his brains rather than his fists to get a job done. The five hundred head of horses he ran on his ranch near Las Cruces gave him enough aches and pains these days for any five men.

"Mr. McQuay," called Jim Simmons, Mary's husband, as he poked his head in the open ranch-house door, "that buckskin is saddled and ready for you."

J.D. slipped six twenty-dollar gold pieces from a pocket and showed the rancher five of them. "A hundred dollars for horse, tack, and the best meal in Texas—I believe that was the agreed price."

"Hundred dollars even was the bargain." Simmons nodded.

J.D. left all six of the gold pieces on the table beside his plate. He told himself it was because Simmons had underpriced the horse, and he did not want to cheat the young rancher. The truth was the Simmonses used their ranch as a stagecoach way station for the extra money it brought in. The couple reminded him of how it had been with Caitlyn and himself at one time, when they had done the same to make ends meet. Once a passing stranger had overtipped them twenty dollars—money that had made the difference in making it through a long, hard, cold winter. Today he repaid that generosity. *You get back what you give,* J.D. thought, as he dropped the extra coin by his empty coffee cup.

Tipping his hat to the lady of the house and shaking her husband's hand, J.D. walked outside and mounted a buckskin gelding that stood seventeen hands at the withers. He nudged the horse into a bouncy jog and then into an easy galloping lope. "Let's go, Gen—"

J.D. caught himself and shook his head. He had forgotten that he had sent General Lee ahead to greet his wife. An amused smile spread across his face. *I'd give another hundred dollars just to see the expression on Cat's face when she opens that stage and finds General Lee grinning up at her.* A long time ago, his wife would have laughed at his little joke. Now he imagined her getting all huffy and indignant, putting on the airs she seemed so fond of—airs he had never understood.

I'll probably get a tongue-lashing to end all tongue-lashings when I reach the Big House. He shook his head. He simply did not know how to judge Cat anymore. He hoped she recognized that General Lee was more than a joke, that the dog was a message telling her that he was on his way to her—in his own way.

Hope he did, but he did not expect that understanding any more than he expected Cat to grasp why he had jumped the stage or taken the time to eat a hearty home-cooked meal before proceeding alone on horseback. He had eaten the meal because he was hungry and was not certain when he would have the opportunity to eat again. J.D. expected no particularly warm welcome with bed and board from Cat. He rode the buckskin to make certain only those he wanted to know knew of his arrival. Cat's telegram, while not specifically spelling out a warning, had caution written between the lines.

J.D.'s fingers moved to a shirt pocket, dug past the reading glasses nestled there, and pulled out Cat's message of alarm. He held the yellow paper at arm's length and, in spite of the buckskin's jostling strides, managed to skim the words he had read at least a hundred times since the wire had reached him in Las Cruces:

Katherine is in trouble. If you are not here in a
week, I will consider you dead.
                Caitlyn Marie Kennedy McQuay

A hint of sadness touched the corners of his mouth as his eyes traced over the way Cat had signed her name— not "your wife, Caitlyn," but "Caitlyn Marie Kennedy McQuay" as though he had to be reminded of the name of the woman he married.

He slipped the telegram back into the pocket and tapped the buckskin's flanks with his heels, urging the horse to a faster trot.

The wire was as enigmatic as Cat herself. It told him nothing, yet at the same time it said everything. Only a life-and-death matter would have motivated Caitlyn to send that wire, especially after their five years of self-imposed separation. The life, in this case, was that of their only child, Katherine—perhaps the one and only reason J.D. would return to Monte Verde. Something he was certain Cat realized.

The serpentine road he followed through the Davis Mountains abruptly ended. Easing back on the reins, he drew the buckskin to a halt and scanned the miles of prairie rolling away like an ocean of grass before him. No more than a black dot amid that green sea was the stagecoach he had jumped off back at the Simmonses'. At least fifteen miles beyond the stage stood Monte Verde, looking no larger or smaller than it had appeared five years ago when J.D. had taken one final glance at the town from this very spot before riding out of Texas and Cat and Katherine's lives. He had thought his departure was forever.

As he tugged the gelding's head to the south, his heels once more nudged the animal's flanks and kept tapping the horse's sides until the buckskin's long legs stretched out in an easy run. Unless Cat had found herself another driver for that fringed surrey she was so fond of, he could easily arrive at the Circle Q even before old Moss managed to bring Cat to the Big House's front door. Even better was the fact that those in Monte Verde would be watching the approaching stage and not a lone rider who swung wide around the town.

J.D. let the buckskin have its head as they crested the gently rolling hill. The horse immediately slowed to a walk and then stopped and dipped its head to the ankle-deep blue grama grass and grazed. Dismounting, J.D. slipped the braided reins over the animal's ears and let the reins drop to the ground. The buckskin had been ridden too long and hard to attempt to run away until it caught its wind. That would be time enough for its rider to gather the myriad of feelings that stirred in his breast.

Turning a full three hundred and sixty degrees, J.D. let his eyes trace over the open prairie that spread like a carpet from horizon to horizon. A chill of excitement coursed up and down his spine—the same sensation he had experienced when he had first come to this land after the Civil War. He had thought five years had separated him well enough from this country, but he was wrong. Here was a lost part of him that his horse ranch in Las Cruces, for all its own beauty, had never been able to replace.

Twenty-five years old. He recalled his age when he had first let his eyes soak in this prairie's majesty. God, it seemed a lifetime away, and yet as though it had happened only yesterday. Wearing a tattered and stained Confederate captain's uniform, he had returned from the Civil War. His childhood sweetheart, Caitlyn Marie Kennedy, a radiant Austin debutante of eighteen when he had marched away to fight for the honor of the South, had been transformed into a woman in full bloom during his five years' absence. When they were reunited, the first words out of his mouth were, "Will you marry me?" And her unequivocal answer was, "Yes."

J.D. had spent five years of his life fighting Union troops on the bloody battlefields of the East. Protracting

the war against the carpetbaggers who later flocked to
Austin held no interest for him. J.D. sold the nearby farm
he had inherited from his father, took the money and his
new bride, and traveled west to Monte Verde, little more
than a trading post in those days.

The only state in the Union to have been a sovereign
nation before being admitted to the United States, Texas
had no government land available to homesteaders. All the
money J.D. and Caitlyn had to their names went to
purchase a one-room sod house, a half section of land, and
a small herd of longhorns.

A distant smile slid across J.D.'s lips as he remembered those wild range cattle. They had meant little to
him when he bought the land, except as a supply of meat
to get Cat and him through their first winter. His plan had
been to work the land as his grandfather, who had been
one of Stephen F. Austin's original colonists, as his father
had before him. He had not reckoned on the taste for
beefsteak the nation had acquired during the long years of
deprivation during the war. He and his longhorns had
been on the first drive along what men now called the
Chisholm Trail.

In the years that followed, that half section of prairie
grew to a full twenty sections and the Circle Q brand
became known as a great ranch throughout Texas. To be
sure, there were larger ranches between the Rio Grande
and the Red River, but few as productive, J.D. recalled
with no small sense of pride.

Looking back on it now, he could not escape the
notion that his accomplishment in those fifteen years had
been nothing short of a miracle. First there had been the
Lipan Apaches and the Comanches, who did their best to
see that a fledgling rancher not only failed in his endeavor,
but was sent to his grave without his scalp. Until '74,
when the U.S. Army caught up with Quanah Parker's band
of Comanches in Palo Duro Canyon, Cat and he had lived
in fear of every full moon, when Comanche raiding parties
thundered out of the northern plains.

Nor were red men his only problem. Those with
white and brown skins also saw the Circle Q as a chance at

quick fortune. J.D. had dealt with what seemed like more than his share of rustlers.

During those years Cat and he had faced and conquered all that Texas had thrown at them, be it drought, outlaws, or Indian raiders. They had built a spread most men and women would have been proud to claim as their own.

Then we did to ourselves what no one else could do. J.D. shook his head in disgust. The Big House had been the start of Cat's putting on airs. Then came an endless stream of high-society guests from Jefferson, Austin, and Houston. The trips to New York, Paris, and London.

It was as though Cat had been trying to recapture the life of a debutante she had known before the war, a time that was as dead to J.D. as were the Apache war chiefs who once claimed this land as their own. He had endured those pretentious guests and Cat's long absences for as long as he could. Then one morning, shortly after Cat had returned from yet another self-indulgent trip to Austin, he had gotten out of bed, thrown a change of clothes into a saddlebag, saddled a horse, and ridden away into freedom, vowing never to return.

Sadly his head moved from side to side. They had been fools, the both of them. Only fools destroy a life such as Cat and he had shared. But like the fools they were, they had chosen their separate paths, and now there was no turning back.

J.D. closed his eyes, filled his lungs, and exhaled. This was not the time for reminiscences or regrets. What had been done was in the past and irretrievable, water over the dam. He had not come to this hill to remember a life that was no longer his, but to pay his respects to his sons.

When his eyes opened, it was not to drink in the vastness of the Circle Q, which ran as far as the eye could see in all directions, but to find two small, well-kept graves farther along the hilltop. Beside them he knelt and said not one, but two prayers for the souls of the infants he had buried here so many years ago.

James Kennedy McQuay, named after Cat's father, had been born to them a year after their marriage. The influenza had taken him during the winter. A year later

Timothy Morgan McQuay came into the world. Two weeks later Cat and J.D. awoke from a night's sleep to find their second son dead in his cradle. They had never even had the cold comfort of learning the cause of his death; they had simply buried him.

Saying his second "Amen," J.D. rose and turned back to the buckskin. After eighteen years something threatened his one remaining child. The thought was intolerable. The time had come for him to answer Cat's telegram.

He gathered the buckskin's reins and looped them again over the animal's head. Thrusting a boot into a stirrup, he swung into the saddle and then reined the weary horse southward toward the Big House. He had a job to do, and do it he would.

Chapter Five

J.D. rode down the white gravel approach to the Big House. Wide enough to accommodate two wagons, the road ended in a sweeping circle in front of a three-story edifice—J.D. found it difficult to think of the Big House anymore as a home—that imitated antebellum plantation mansions, Doric columns and all. Easing the buckskin to a halt before the massive mahogany door, J.D. dismounted and tied the gelding's reins to a black-lacquered cast-iron hitching post in the shape of a horse's head.

Cat had seen the hitching posts during her first visit to the elegant French Quarter in New Orleans and had ordered a dozen to be stationed in front of her own home. The twelve posts still stood, looking like a dozen knights abducted from a chess board, impaled on top of iron pikes.

After giving the doorbell three good twists, J.D. rapped his knuckles against the mahogany to make doubly certain those inside the immense house heard him. A full minute passed before the door opened to reveal a gray-haired man in the white jacket of a servant.

"Moss?" J.D. blinked in surprise and did his best to suppress the smile that spread across his lips. "What in blazes are you doing in that outfit?"

Moss glanced down and pressed imagined wrinkles from the lapels of the linen jacket. "This here is my official manservant—" His words faltered and his head snapped up. For an instant he squinted at J.D., and then his eyes flew wide and an ear-to-ear grin stretched across his wrinkled face. "Mac? Is that really you, boss?"

"It's me all right."

Moss's hand shot out, grabbed J.D.'s right, and vigorously pumped up and down. "I'll be a coon-tailed dog. I never thought I'd live to see the day that—" Moss's expression grew as stern as a Baptist preacher's on Sunday morning. "What are you doin' here? Don't you know that Miss Caitlyn's promised to skin you alive if you ever stepped foot in this house again? If she finds out you're here, she'll—"

"It's all right, Moss. Caitlyn sent for me." After he had pulled up stakes and headed for the New Mexico Territory, J.D. realized, Cat had most likely threatened to do far worse to him when and if they met again. "Why don't you tell her the man of the house has come home?"

Dubiously, Moss nodded. "If that's what you want, Mac. But remember I done warned you."

J.D. smiled as he watched the old wrangler disappear down the entry hall. Moss had once been the best bronc-buster in the Southwest, until he ran into a walleyed sorrel mustang that tossed him on his head and then proceeded to do the Mexican hat dance on his belly. The throw had been a nasty one, resulting in two broken legs, a shattered arm, and a fractured skull. The broken legs and arm had eventually healed. Not so with Moss's head. The accident left him with half the sense God had given him at birth. J.D. had first given Moss his job as Cat's surrey driver. It was to her credit that she had kept him on. A man like Moss deserved the dignity of real employment no matter how simple he seemed these days.

Cleaning the bottom of his boots on a scrape set in the ground beside the front steps, J.D. entered the cool house. The smell of lemon oil wafted in his nostrils. He smiled; the fragrance was one of the few things he had ever liked about the Big House. The redolence of polished walls and furniture always seemed warm and friendly, like the rich aroma of brewing coffee when friends are gathered around a kitchen table.

"Miss Caitlyn says I'm to bring you straight away into the study." Moss had returned, his head waggling in disbelief. "Says she been expectin' you. Strange, she never let on how she was thinkin' you'd show up here."

"Don't let it worry your mind, Moss. There's a lot of

things Caitlyn doesn't let on." J.D. motioned for the man to lead him to the inner sanctum where the power of this house, Caitlyn, awaited him.

Down the walnut-paneled hallway they walked, past rooms cluttered with fancy furniture she had imported from England, Germany, France, and Italy. J.D. tried to repress the cold shiver that shot up his spine, and failed. While he could appreciate fine things, no naturally born man could ever feel comfortable in such lavish surroundings. There was no place he could stretch out his legs without the fear he might scratch or break something.

"I know what she said." Moss stopped before the double doors to the study. "But to be on the safe side, I think it would be best if you let yourself in while I put myself at the other end of the house."

With that Moss turned tail and scuttled away, casting one dubious glance back at J.D.

J.D. watched his old friend scurry to safety for a moment and then faced the closed door of the study. An involuntary quiver trembled through his body; whether it stemmed from Moss's actions or his own uncertainty, he was not sure. After all, five years was a long time. He could only guess at Cat's reaction to seeing him again. Half the mental images those guesses evoked rivaled the gruesome tortures Comanches once performed on their captives. Caitlyn's temper was as Irish as her name and the fiery red of her hair.

Steeling himself for the worst, J.D. heaved a deep breath, reached out, opened the doors, stepped inside the study, and closed the doors behind him without ever letting his gaze lift from the polished hardwood floor. When he did—

Caitlyn stood beside a mahogany desk in a pale green silk dress with accents of delicate lace around the neck and wrists. Her head turned. Those emerald green eyes alighted on J.D. and fixed him in place.

General Lee stood at her side. The dog lifted its head to acknowledge J.D.'s presence, but remained with Caitlyn.

He swallowed hard, like an itchy grammar-school boy who found himself beneath the Christmas mistletoe with the prettiest girl in the class. Only Caitlyn was not just pretty—she was beautiful. If anything, she was far more beautiful than the image he had carried in his mind for five years. Nor was Caitlyn a girl; she was a woman. Just how much a woman was something he had never forgotten, nor was he ever likely to forget.

A smile that contained something more than the relief of a distraught mother in it brightened her face. Her voice came soft and gentle when she spoke. "Jonathan."

To others, friends and acquaintances, he was either J.D. or Mac. Or, as the case had become far too often in the past years, "Mr. McQuay." As respectful as it was, the utterance also was a constant reminder of the years that weighed on his shoulders. Caitlyn was the only one who ever used his Christian name, the only person from whom he enjoyed hearing that word.

"Cat." J.D. tugged his hat from his head. Without conscious thought his arms opened to her, ready to squeeze tightly about her slender waist in a homecoming embrace.

Her own arms lifted, and she took two steps toward him. Then she abruptly halted. Her eyes narrowed, and her back stiffened as though an invisible steel brace had snapped tight along her spine.

"Jonathan." The warmth evaporated from her tone when she repeated his name; the all-too-familiar cold formality was back. "Your messenger arrived earlier today, but he was unable to impart the exact time you would grace us with your presence."

She glanced down at General Lee to make certain J.D. understood her meaning. With a wave of a hand, she signaled the dog to return to his rightful owner. General Lee stared up at her with a canine imitation of a human grin on his face, but did not move.

"You're looking good, Cat." J.D. ignored the frosty edge in her voice. He had caught a glimmer of something in her eyes he had wanted to see for longer than he liked to remember, something he wanted to pursue. "The years haven't touched you. You're still a handsome woman."

Her face softened and her lips parted as though to accept the compliment—for the space of two heartbeats. Then the rigidity overtook her face and body again. "I didn't summon you here to discuss my appearance, but to ask your assistance in an urgent matter concerning my daughter, who by accident of birth also happens to be your child."

J.D. let the term "summon" slide by. That was just Cat and her airs. But he could not do the same with her last comment. "Katherine's *our* daughter—her birth was not an accident. If I recall rightly, the effort required to bring her into the world came with our mutual consent and *pleasure.*"

A hint of red tinged Caitlyn's cheeks. Whether from anger or embarrassment, he could not be certain. Nor did she give him the opportunity to find out. She switched back to her original angle of attack without batting an eyelash.

"I expected you on the noon stage that I had specially arranged for you at great personal inconvenience and some expense. You, however, preferred to make a fool out of me by sending a dog in your stead."

J.D. bit his lower lip and let the obvious canine remarks pass. In a matter of a few minutes, Cat and he had returned to where they had stood five years ago. He had not traveled all the way from Las Cruces to resume this petty bickering. "I received your wire, and I came. From the tone of your message, I figured that Katherine was in some danger. Working on that, and the assumption you wanted me here because you felt that I could do some good, I came in the way *I* felt would do the most good. The fewer people who realize that I'm here the better. It will allow me room to move around more freely."

He paused to let Caitlyn answer. When she did not, he continued. "You didn't say much in your telegram, Cat. You do want me here, don't you?"

"Of course I want you here. Why else would I have sent that wire?" She blinked as though uncertain how to deal with him. "I couldn't say more in the telegram, Jonathan. I didn't want the whole country to know what has happened. As it is, everyone in Monte Verde already knows and probably half of Presidio County, too." Her voice quavered, and she shuddered. "Katherine . . . Katherine has been kidnapped."

"Kidnapped?" J.D. stared at her, unsure he heard correctly.

"Three days ago, seven men took her from a stagecoach as it passed through the Del Norte Mountains. They killed the stage's guard for no good reason and seriously wounded one of the passengers." Caitlyn took a yellow sheet of paper from the desktop and handed it to J.D. "These are their demands."

Even holding the paper at arm's length, J.D. found the writing too blurred to read. He pulled a pair of wire-rimmed spectacles from his shirt pocket and clamped them to his nose. They were a recent concession to his aging eyesight, and from the corner of an eye he saw exasperation darken Caitlyn's face. The moment was too anxious for him to ask whether she was impatient with his need for his spectacles or with the illegibility of the outlaw's scrawl. He ignored her look and began reading. A whistle escaped his lips. "Half a million dollars? Have you got that much to your name?"

"Thank God, yes. After you left, I expanded our interests into railroads, mines, stocks and bonds, and even bought a few small stagecoach lines," she said. "I'm having to liquidate most everything there is, except of course the Circle Q, to do it, but with the bankers' help I've managed to come up with the ransom money."

Pointing behind J.D., she directed his gaze to an oversized trunk. "It's all in gold coin, just to be on the safe side. Twenty-dollar pieces. Bank notes make some men balk. You know better than I that there are still plenty of towns out here on the range where a fistful of paper bills won't even buy you a cup of coffee. And the closer to Mexico you are, the truer this is. You've got eight days to deliver the money into their hands down in—"

"Presidio," he finished for her as he read the last words of the ransom note. "The eight days that remain are more than enough time to make it. At least time is in our favor."

He walked to the chest and opened it. Another low whistle escaped his lips as he stared at the fortune amassed in that single chest. "A man could run a small country on this much money. Is this all of—"

"No, the bulk of it is in our cellar vault. Five hundred thousand is astonishing, I know, but it's what they demanded. It's what you will deliver," she answered.

J.D.'s right eyebrow arched high when he looked back at his wife. "Just to make certain we understand each other, Cat, do I have this right? You want me to handle this situation in the way I see fit?"

Caitlyn's green eyes lowered to the floor, and she nibbled at her lower lip for several long seconds before her chest heaved and she looked up to nod. "There's no one else I can trust with Katherine's life. You may use your own discretion to work this out in any manner you see fit, as long as you bring our daughter back here unharmed."

It was J.D.'s turn to nod. They understood each other, and he *would* handle the situation in his own way. "I'll want to get started tomorrow morning, if I can arrange all that I need tonight."

"I've already gathered the supplies you'll need—food, water bags, pistols, rifles, shotguns, and ammunition for all—enough for ten men," Caitlyn said.

"I'll only need enough for two men on the way down and three counting Katherine, for the return trip," J.D. replied immediately.

"Two men?" Caitlyn started to protest, but then caught herself. She had given him free rein to run this show as he saw fit. "Then I'll make sure you have enough for four men, just to be on the safe side."

J.D. nodded his agreement. "And I'll need this gold broken up and put into smaller boxes—not too big to be carried on the backs of mules." His eyes reflected his quick calculation and planning. "And the mules to carry the boxes, of course."

"Of course." She tilted her head in agreement. "Everything will be ready when you are."

"Tomorrow at sunup," J.D. said. "I'll leave then. The sooner I get this gold down to Presidio the better I'll feel."

He tried not to consider the many hard miles of prairie, mountains, and desert that lay between him and the border town. With a train of mules heavily laden with gold, he would be lucky to make twenty, maybe twenty-five, miles a day.

"Then you'll want a good night's sleep before you leave." Caitlyn's tone indicated there was nothing left for them to say. "I've had a room prepared for you."

"If it's the master bedroom, neither one of us will get much rest tonight." He grinned and lifted his eyebrows suggestively.

She tried to ignore the remark, though J.D. could see that she was momentarily excited, in spite of herself, by his bold implication, particularly at a moment of crisis and after so long an absence. But she quickly mastered herself. "No, J.D.," she said coldly. "A guest bedroom."

"Then I'll have to turn it down. I have three days worth of things to get done before dawn." He shrugged and his eyebrows drooped in obvious disappointment. "I'll need a couple of good horses and saddles."

"Moss will go with you to the barn. Take whatever you need."

J.D. snapped his fingers to bring General Lee to his side. He then turned to the doors and reached for their silver knobs. He paused and glanced over his shoulder. "Cat, you get some rest. I'll find Katherine, you can bet on that, and I'll bring her back to you."

He did not wait for a reply, but stepped into the hall and called for Moss.

Caitlyn listened to his footsteps and the pad of General Lee's paws receding on the polished tile floor. Moving to the nearest chair, she sank into it. For three days she had managed this insane affair and held back her own emotions. At last she buried her face in her hands and broke down and cried. Everything now rested on the shoulders of the only man she had ever fully trusted—the only man she had ever loved.

Chapter Six

Monte Verde drifted in the drowsy state that hovers over all small towns between the last cup of after-dinner coffee and the puff of breath extinguishing the bedroom candle. Here and there kerosene lights glowed yellow from the windows of houses that J.D. passed as he rode into town astride a midnight-black gelding with a single white star on its forehead. On his right, J.D. led a saddled and bridled bay filly. Quietly moving on his left was General Lee, with ears perked and eyes alert.

He was grateful for the night. With the town near slumber there were no eyes to see the riderless horse nor mouths to question either the filly's or his own suspicious presence in Monte Verde. Half a million dollars was a heavy burden to be placed in anyone's lap, and he would just as well keep his movements as quiet as possible.

Avoiding Monte Verde's main street and the light from a cantina, the only business establishment open in town after sundown, he reined his mount behind a low-slung structure built of native Texas granite. He dismounted and tied the reins of the gelding and filly to the branches of a live oak that grew beside the building. A simple hand signal commanded General Lee to stand guard with the horses.

J.D. glanced about. If he was being watched, the eyes that followed him were well hidden. Long, quick strides brought him to the front of the solid rock building. The yellow light of lamps within cast a soft glow across a wooden shingle hung crookedly above the door. It bore a

single word—JAIL—in sun-bleached paint. J.D. opened
the door and walked in without knocking.

A young man, who leaned back in a chair against a
wall, lifted the downturned brim of his hat, glanced at
J.D. and then called to an open door that led back to the
jail's cells. "Pa, we got company." When he glanced back
at the visitor, he pushed the chair from the wall and stood
up straight. "Friend, I have the distinct feeling that you
and I have met before."

When J.D. had last set eyes on Harlan Brewster, he
had been a lanky and awkward kid, not the full-grown,
good-looking man now before him, a deputy sheriff's badge
pinned to his chest. "The name's—"

"J.D. McQuay!" Els Brewster called out as he walked
into the office. The sheriff stuck out a hand.

"Els, I see the years haven't made you any handsomer."
J.D. shook his old friend's hand and then extended a hand
to Harlan.

"Mr. McQuay, it's good to see you again. I'm sorry I
didn't recognize you right off," Harlan apologized with a
chagrined expression on his face.

"No reason for you to recognize me. It's been five
years since we last saw each other. That's a lot of water
under the bridge, and enough time for a boy to grow up
and grow hair all over." J.D. smiled and shook his head.
"To be honest I almost didn't recognize you myself."

"I reckon I don't have to ask what brings you back to
Monte Verde." Els cut the reunion pleasantries short.
"Have you talked with Caitlyn?"

J.D. pursed his lips and tilted his head. "She filled
me in on all that's happened. I'm to take the ransom to
Presidio."

Els's face grew somber, and he rubbed a hand over
his neck. "I did my damnedest to find them that took
Katherine, J.D., but they laid about a score of false trails.
Got so they had me and my posse ridin' 'round in circles."

"This wasn't some spur-of-the-moment thing, Mr.
McQuay," Harlan said when his father fell into embarrassed
silence. "The men who kidnapped your daughter had
everything planned out. They were ready for every move
we made."

"Nobody's calling fault," J.D. said. "You did what you could."

"Which wasn't enough." Bitterness tainted Els's voice. "That's why Caitlyn sent for you."

J.D. had no intention of pointing a finger of accusation at his longtime friend. "She wired for me because Katherine is my daughter, and I have a right to be here."

Els said nothing as he moved behind the desk, settled into a chair, and motioned for J.D. to pull up another.

J.D. did, staring across the desk at his friend. "Surely someone around here has seen something. Seven men riding on the West Texas prairie with a young woman would be pretty hard to miss."

"It's a big country, J.D." Els shook his head. "A twister could cut a mile-wide path through parts of the county and nobody would even notice."

"We're not talking about a tornado. These are seven men with an eighteen-year-old girl as a captive. And they're on their way to Presidio. Seems to me that narrows the area to search down to a specific route."

"I've wired the Presidio authorities to keep an eye out for any strangers who might be slinkin' around in their town. I've also sent riders out to alert ranchers south of here to be on the lookout for seven men ridin' with a young woman," Els tried to reassure him. "I see the situation the same way you do."

"The rangers don't," Harlan interrupted.

"Rangers?" J.D.'s head snapped around, and he glared at the young man. "What rangers?"

"Texas Rangers, of course," Harlan answered.

"Rangers?" This time J.D. aimed the question at Els. "You didn't go and call the rangers in on this, did you?"

"There ain't no finer lawmen in all of Texas, J.D., and you know that. If anybody can find Katherine, it will be these two rangers that come in from San Angelo," Els said. "I talked with them this very afternoon. They think they might have somethin'."

"Rangers." J.D. sank back in his chair, making no effort to hide his disgust. He respected the Texas Rangers as much as any man. The wire Els had to send to get them here had certainly spread word of Katherine's kidnapping across half the state. The more people who knew about the huge gold ransom, the more complicated delivering that ransom would be.

"The rangers don't think the kidnappers have taken Katherine south to Presidio yet," Harlan said. "They believe someone would have noticed them if they had. They're working with the view that instead of riding south after taking Katherine off the stagecoach, they found themselves someplace around here to hole up. That way they cut down the possibility of running into a posse."

J.D. shook his head and fixed his gaze on his friend. "I don't give a damn what two Texas Rangers I've never laid eyes on before think happened. This is my daughter we're talking about. I want them pulled off this case immediately. Caitlyn has put the ransom together; don't ask me how. Sold off practically everything we had. I'll handle this the way Caitlyn wants it done—the way I want it done. I'll get Katherine back, and I'll do it my way."

"Your way?" Els glowered at J.D. in disbelief. "Do you have any idea how many people already know about that ransom money Caitlyn's been raisin'? You can't spend two days jumpin' in and out of this town's only bank and telegraph office and then send three wagons to pick up a huge load of coins, thousands of pounds' worth, without expectin' to attract people's attention."

"Well, Els, there's a damn sight more folks know what's up now than would have if you hadn't called in the Texas Rangers," J.D. said, feeling his temper begin to rise.

Els did not listen. "Anyone tryin' to carry half a million dollars to Presidio without a small army ridin' guard with him is only invitin' his own death."

"That's my problem to worry about," J.D. answered coolly. "If trouble comes up, I'll handle it in my own style, like I've always done."

Harlan cleared his throat and stepped beside the desk so that he faced J.D. squarely. "Texas has changed, Mr. McQuay. Things ain't the way they used to be. A man doesn't take the law into his own hands here these days. We have duly sworn officers to protect the citizens of Texas now. My advice is for you to forget whatever plan it is you have in your mind and ride back out to the Circle Q and let the law handle whatever needs to be done. We'll get your daughter back."

J.D. shoved from his chair. He did his best to hold himself under control. "Son, the law doesn't seem to be doing a whole lot, the way I see it." He looked at Els. "That he's your son, Els, is the only thing that's stopping me from giving your deputy's nose a rude introduction to my fist, then dusting off the seat of his pants with my size eleven boot."

"J.D., there's no need to get all worked up." Els tried to calm his friend.

"Mr. McQuay, I didn't mean to offend you," Harlan started in again, but was waved to silence by his father.

"Why don't you sit back down in that chair and let's talk this through?" Els continued.

J.D.'s gaze shifted between father and son. "The only thing I need from either of you right now is for one of you to tell me where I can find Reb Boggs."

"Reb Boggs? Why would you want to find that old horse thief?" Harlan's face twisted in disdain.

"He's still livin' in that old shack up in the Davis Mountains," Els answered. "But he ain't the man he used to be when you knew him, J.D. He's changed. Half the ranchers in this county would be happy to see him danglin' from the wrong end of a hangman's rope."

The concerns of half the county were of no matter to J.D. He tipped his hat to the two men. He then turned and walked to the door. Evidently nothing more could be gained here, and a long night of hard riding lay before him if he were to be back at the Circle Q by sunup.

"J.D., I can't stop you from doing what you've a mind to do," Els said behind him. "But I have to warn you that if you do anything outside the law, I'll have to come after you, too. It's like Harlan said. Things have changed in these parts."

J.D. turned and glanced back at his friend. A barrage of appropriate curses formed in his mind, but he left them unspoken. "Things might have changed, but I haven't."

Opening the door, J.D. stepped back into the night.

*   *   *

A moon three days short of full hung in the clear West
Texas sky. Its light illuminated the Davis Mountains like a
frosty sun. Although this was 1885 and the days of Comanche
raids lay more than a decade in the past, J.D. found
himself haunted by old doubts and fears.

The two weeks of each month when the moonlight
cast its twilight glow across prairie and mountain had once
been known throughout Texas as the time of the Blood
Moon. For younger Texans, those who had never lived
through nights of half-sleep plagued by sounds a man was
certain were made by raiding Comanches and their Kiowa
allies approaching his home, the soul-shattering terror of
the Blood Moon was only a disembodied reminiscence, a
story told by fathers and grandfathers.

But to one who had lived through those terrifying
nights, they remained real, and old images were impossible to shake clear from the mind. Even the Apaches of the
New Mexico Territory, fierce warriors though they were,
had never set such ice floes coursing through J.D.'s veins.
The Apaches feared the night and fought only by the light
of day. The Comanches were worse: Always a threat in
sunlight, they completely dominated the nights of the
Blood Moon.

Twenty-five feet ahead of J.D., General Lee abruptly
stopped. A low growl came from the dog's throat. His
head swung to the right, and his ears pointed to a clump
of bushy junipers.

J.D. drew back on the black gelding's reins. His own
head cocked to one side as he, too, listened. Nothing, he
heard nothing. Which did not lessen his apprehension. He
rode with General Lee—had ridden with four General
Lees before this one—because a dog heard and smelled
things a man's senses missed.

As suddenly as he had stopped, General Lee moved
forward again.

Nudging the gelding after the dog, J.D. slowly released a long breath. Whatever the dog had heard was
gone now. In all likelihood it had been a jackrabbit or
maybe a larger denizen of these mountains, such as a mule
deer or a pronghorn antelope. Had it been a predator like
a mountain lion, General Lee would never have started

along the path they followed again. He would have waited until J.D. disposed of the danger threatening them, or would have attempted to do so himself.

J.D.'s gaze lifted, tracing along the narrow, twisting route they traveled. It wound like a snake halfway up the side of a grass-covered mountain where it disappeared into a cedar brake. Unlike other mountains, those of the Big Bend region produced a reverse timberline. Stunted trees and bushes grew near the crests instead of around the base.

The explanation for this strange behavior was simple. The Big Bend region of Texas was basically dry lands, in spite of the brief, explosive rainstorms that drenched the plains during the summer. However, moisture-bearing clouds pushed out of Mexico all year round, often traveling hundreds of miles to north-central Texas before releasing that precious rain. Most of these clouds brushed the tops of the Davis Mountains on their journey northward. It was from their foggy, misty bodies that the junipers and pines up high sucked the moisture they needed to live.

Amid the dense cedar brake that J.D. was now approaching, Reb Boggs had built the shack he called home when he had come to this region. His given reason for the mountain dwelling was that, although relatively exposed in plain sight, its remote location and difficult access made it a poor target for Indian attack.

The truth of the matter, as J.D. and everyone in the area were well aware, was that Reb had a fondness for corn squeezings. Even when Reb had served as an Indian scout for the army, he had managed to keep a still operating on his mountainside, producing some of the sweetest white lightning J.D. had ever tasted.

Tonight, J.D. was not seeking out the old Indian fighter, who had befriended Caitlyn and him their first year in Presidio County, for a gallon of moonshine. When it came to tracking and the ability to live off the land, no man alive could outdo Reb, unless he had been born with full Comanche or Apache blood. For what lay ahead, J.D. needed such a man at his side.

A throaty growl came from ahead once again. J.D. halted his mount. General Lee stood at the edge of the cedar brake, ears pinned back and teeth exposed in a feral snarl. No rabbit or deer ever caused the dog to react so. J.D.'s right hand reached for the Winchester in his saddle holster.

A rifle barked. Blue and yellow flame blazed from somewhere inside the brake. Before J.D. heard its whine, hot lead slapped into the crown of his hat, tugged it from his head, and sent it flying through the air.

"Get them hands up in plain sight, or I'll put the next one right between your ugly eyes," a gravelly voice called out.

J.D. did as ordered.

"Now call the dog. I ain't of a mind to kill no dog tonight," the voice demanded.

Again J.D. complied. "General Lee, here."

The dog immediately trotted back and sat on his haunches beside the gelding. But the low growl continued to rumble in his throat.

"General Lee?" A hint of puzzlement echoed in the gravelly voice. "You got a name, stranger?"

"It would have been a whole lot easier if you'd asked for it first instead of trying to blow my head off, Reb Boggs." J.D. made no attempt to hide his disgust.

"I'll still take your head off your shoulders, if you don't give me a civil answer—and be quick about it."

"McQuay," J.D. answered. "J.D. McQuay."

There was a moment's silence before the voice replied with an undertone of mirth. "You're pushing your luck, stranger. J.D. McQuay ain't been seen in this country for a coon's age. And if he was stupid enough to show his face 'round here, he wouldn't last for more'n a few minutes 'fore that redheaded she-demon he calls a wife flayed the hide offa him."

"You ought to know, since you almost lost your own hide to her the day you tried to steal that apple pie Cat set in the window to cool."

A pleased laugh rippled from the cedars. "Caitlyn sure as hell was mad over that, weren't she? Wouldn't speak to me for a month or more."

J.D. grinned, recalling his wife's anger. "If you've had

your fun, can I put my hands down and pick up the hat you just ruined?"

"Do that and come on up to the clearing. I got a bit of heaven on earth rollin' out of the coil right now. We'll share a taste or two."

There was a rustle of branches as Reb retreated into the cedars. J.D. stepped from the saddle and found his hat twenty feet downhill. Reb's shot had been placed squarely at the tip of the creased crown. His old friend might have changed as Els had said, but he had not lost his eye. That was a good sign, especially for what J.D. had in mind as this week's work.

Reb waited in the clearing behind his shack with two tin cups in hand. He handed one to J.D. and then watched with expectation as his friend sampled the offering. Although the corn liquor was only seconds old and burned more than a little as it went down, J.D. managed to smack his lips with relish. He voiced a long, satisfied "ahhhhhh." Reb grinned from ear to ear with obvious pleasure and then waved to J.D. to seat himself on a boulder.

"Ain't no better shine made in all of Texas, though there be some who do their damnedest to shut me down." Reb took a healthy swallow from his own cup. "When I saw you comin' up the mountain, I thought you might be—"

"Els Brewster?" J.D. studied the old Indian fighter as he sampled the white lightning again. The second sip went down smoother, or maybe the first sampling had cauterized his throat.

Reb hiked an eyebrow, then shook his head. "Els ain't that bad, I reckon. Though I can't say the same for that wet-behind-the-ears son of his. Harlan takes his sheriffin' a mite serious."

J.D. pursed his lips. "From what I hear, you might have something to do with that."

Five years had not left Reb unchanged. The salt-and-pepper hair J.D. remembered was now snow-white. And somewhere along the way Reb had lost his acquaintance with a razor. Whiskers as white as the strands on his head covered his face. Although standing only an inch under

J.D.'s own six feet, Reb looked smaller than J.D. recalled. Perhaps it was because the old scout had grown gaunt and wiry with the years.

Finishing off his cup, Reb licked his lips and shrugged. "I ain't sayin' I ain't never bent a law or five, J.D., but it ain't me that's changed. I keep livin' the way I always done. It's this country. Hell, a man can't spit on a town street no more without someone wantin' to slap him in jail for defacin' public property."

J.D. glanced down to hide his smile. When Reb bent the law, it usually was five at the same time. The way his friend had kept living was mostly off the plentiful game in these mountains, but he had been known to claim more than one stray cow or steer as his own, no matter the brand on the animal. Although it was horses, especially those on the open range, that were more likely to draw Reb's attention—with the same wanton disregard to brands.

The wide loop Reb threw once had been ignored by ranchers and townsfolk, who valued the man's rifle and skill as a fighter in an emergency more than they cared about a few missing head of stock. Now that the Indian threat in Texas was nothing more than a page in the history books, Reb's ways of keeping alive became less admissible each day.

J.D. understood the new attitude and in his mind agreed with it. After all, taming this land was what he and the others had come here to do. But still, in his heart he felt a hollow ache. Texas would be poorer than it once had been when there was no longer a natural place for feisty men like Reb Boggs within her borders.

"Reckon I know what brought you here." Reb found himself a boulder and sat down to face J.D. "It's about little Katherine, ain't it?"

"She isn't little anymore. She's a young woman of eighteen." J.D. nodded. "And I need your help in getting her back."

Reb's lips puckered and a soft whistle escaped them. "I was afraid of that. It ain't goin' to be easy." J.D. took satisfied note that without the need for any persuasion, Reb was already on his side. Reb continued, "You know that, don't you? If an old hermit like me's heard about the half million in gold them desperadoes want for her return, you can bet a lot of unsavory lowlifes have too. And they'll be fixin' to relieve you of that money 'fore you ever get it anywheres near Presidio."

"Els Brewster hasn't helped that situation any. He's called in the rangers."

Reb stroked his whiskers and shook his head sadly. "Els, as good a man as he's always been, never was one for usin' the brains the good Lord gave him."

"If you feel up to it, it'll be just you and me, and of course, General Lee, making the trip down to the border," J.D. said.

That comment arched one of Reb's white eyebrows high. "What you're askin' is for me to make myself a target for every gun in this part of Texas who thinks he's mean enough to take that fortune from us."

"That's right. That's what I'm asking," J.D. agreed.

"And if I somehow managed not to get myself picked off by one of those guns, you're askin' me to get my brains fried to a crisp in the desert durin' the day and freeze my backside off at night. And if by some miracle we do make it all the way to Presidio, we're goin' to be sittin' targets for seven down-and-dirty hombres that probably ain't never even considered actually turnin' Katherine loose once we bring 'em the ransom." Reb stroked his beard and eyed his friend. "Reckon only a crazy man would even think about tryin' to get himself kilt in so many ways. And all in one short week."

J.D. shrugged. "How crazy are you?"

Reb glanced at the still, taking a moment to think. "You know I've had it right easy the past few years, just sittin' here milkin' dew out of this copper contraption." He looked back at J.D. "But I reckon if you're crazy enough to want an old coot like me backin' you up, then I'm crazy enough to tag along. Hell, I never was one for the quiet life, no ways."

Lifting his cup to toast his friend, J.D. said, "To the crazy men of this world." He downed the last of the moonshine; by now it tasted as smooth as aged Kentucky bourbon.

"When you plannin' on us gettin' started?"

"Sunup."

Reb chewed pensively at his lower lip. "Not that it matters none, mind you, but will there be anythin' in it for me?"

"Not that it matters," J.D. answered, "but two hundred dollars seems like a fair price to me."

"I'd rather have a good horse and saddle out of it." Reb cocked his head to one side and stared at his friend.

"That bay filly and the tack on her are yours." J.D. did not have time to go through the amenities of horse trading. "That's on top of the two hundred. If that filly doesn't suit you, then you can have your pick of the stock back at the Circle Q."

A wide grin split Reb's face. "Hell, boy, why you sittin' there on your butt? We got a heap of ridin' to do if we plan to make it back to the Circle Q 'fore first light."

Chapter Seven

"This ain't no time for bull, Dwayne!" Tate Lansdale glared at the young gunman.

"And I ain't throwin' no bull," Dwayne Holt replied. "That sheriff in Monte Verde has brought in the rangers." Holt contained the smile that pulled at his lips. Even in the moonlight he saw the fear on Lansdale's face. Maybe years ago Lansdale had been a top dog, but those days were long past. Now he was nothing more than an old man.

At least thirty, Holt thought. That meant that he was nine years younger and faster than Lansdale. When the time came for them to face each other over the girl and the money, those nine years would make the difference. It would not be like it had been the other night when Lansdale had crept up on him while he was trying to convince the McQuay girl to be friendly. Once Lansdale was neatly out of the way, Holt calculated, he would have the girl to himself and a bigger cut of the ransom.

"Texas Rangers! Son of a bitch!" Lansdale's brain churned, his thoughts clouded by the panic that squeezed around his chest. He had anticipated a posse's attempting to ride them down, but he had never considered the rangers being called in.

"You sure about rangers bein' after us?" Hank Yoakum asked.

Todd Carter joined in. "Yeah, nobody never said nothin' about no rangers bein' brought in. A jerkwater sheriff is one thing, but Texas Rangers is another. I ain't got no want to tangle with the rangers."

"That sheriff can't be that stupid!" Lansdale refused to believe what he heard. "Don't he know we'll kill the girl if we're pressed too much?"

"There's rangers all right. Two of 'em. The whole town of Monte Verde knows about 'em," Holt said, enjoying watching Lansdale squirm. The big brain of this job had missed something, and now he was sweating out his mistake. "I even saw 'em meetin' with the sheriff just before sundown. They was the two men we saw snoopin' 'round down in the pass this mornin'."

Think! Lansdale forced his mind to stop its wild spinning. He had to think this through and get everything straight. He had overlooked a possibility, but that still did not mean he had failed—not as long as they stayed one step ahead of the rangers.

After sighting the two men in the pass this morning, he had sent Holt into town to get a handle on what was happening. He had expected the man to return with word of Caitlyn McQuay's success in raising the ransom and word of when it would be transported to Presidio. Also, he had hoped Holt would find some saloon girl to sate his lust and get the gunman's mind off Katherine McQuay's body. He had never expected him to return with this news.

"Heard a couple ranchers talkin' in a cantina," Holt added. "Seems them rangers ain't so certain that whoever it was that kidnapped the girl has already lit out for Presidio. They think that maybe they're hidin' in these very mountains."

"What're we goin' to do, Tate?"

The lily-livered whine in Kelly Carter's voice grated in Lansdale's ears. "What we don't do is start actin' like a bunch of damned fools. There's too much at stake. Ain't none of us goin' to ever get a chance at a cool half million again in this life."

"Tate's right." This from Ray Powell. "Quiet down and listen to him. He's done all right by us this far. I'm all for lettin' him call the shots."

"The rangers ain't found us yet. What we got to do is make sure it stays that way." Lansdale did not like being pushed into a move, but with rangers involved a man took action while he had the chance or he ended up dead. "All we're goin' to do is step up our plans a mite. We'll start south for Presidio tonight and let them damned rangers search these mountains all they want."

"Tonight?" Billy Crow asked incredulously.

"Soon as we can get mounted," Lansdale ordered. He was back in command. "Ray, wake up the girl and get her on a horse. The rest of you get your gear together. Make it quick."

Fifteen minutes later Tate Lansdale led the way cautiously down the mountain. Reaching the pass below, he headed south. Time and again he glanced nervously over his shoulder. That he saw nothing did not ease the sensation that unseen eyes were watching his every movement.

J.D. tightened the cinch to the gray's saddle, slapped an open palm against the horse's belly, and then drew the surcingle tighter when the animal expelled the air it had used to bloat its belly. He then checked each of the gelding's hooves to make certain the iron shoes it wore would last during the rocky miles ahead.

"Caitlyn said she had new shoes put on these horses last night." Reb eyed his friend skeptically, but J.D. noticed the man also checked how the roan he had chosen had been shod, and then did likewise with the two spare mounts they would take with them.

Lifting a pair of double-barreled twelve-gauge shotguns that leaned against a stall door, J.D. buried one at the center of the sleeping roll tied behind his saddle and passed the other to Reb, who did the same.

"I'm carryin' so much hardware I feel like I'm about to refight the battle of Shiloh all by my lonesome." Reb tucked the ends of his sleeping roll around the butt of the shotgun to make certain it was hidden.

"We might have to do just that before we reach Presidio." There was no trace of humor in J.D.'s voice.

He expected the worst and was prepared for it. Besides the shotguns, he and Reb carried two handguns each, Colt .45s in holsters and Wesson .32s tucked beneath their belts at the small of their backs. Both wore lightweight jackets to hide the latter. In their saddle boots were Winchesters, and J.D. carried a derringer in the top of his right boot. Both men had hunting knives sheathed on their belts and spare blades in their saddlebags.

Behind the four horses, two strings of five mules filled the barn's stables. J.D. moved down one string checking the tack on each animal, while Reb did the same with the second string. Nine of the ten animals carried two wooden boxes each on their backs. They were heavily laden but could handle it. Eighteen triply padlocked boxes in all were required to carry five hundred thousand dollars in gold coin. The tenth mule was loaded down with water bags, supplies, and ammunition.

"It all looks as good as it's going to get," Reb said when he reached the last mule in his string. "Too bad I didn't know you was goin' to need mules. I know where I could've got you ten mules as good as these for a real cheap price."

J.D. did not ask Reb whom he had intended to steal the animals from. He did not want to know.

"Jonathan." Caitlyn stood at the barn, carrying a basket under her arm. "I thought you might like something to eat. It's not much, just some ham-and-egg sandwiches and a jug of hot coffee."

His eyes widening in surprise, J.D. smiled. "It's appreciated, Cat. This might be the last hot meal Reb and I have until Katherine's safe."

"I didn't like the idea of either of you riding out on an empty stomach." She took two napkin-wrapped sandwiches from the basket and handed them to J.D.

"The idea didn't sit none too well with my stomach neither." Reb hastened beside Caitlyn and accepted two sandwiches. "You don't happen to got a piece of that apple pie you make hidden away in that basket, do you?"

Caitlyn chuckled, obviously remembering another apple pie that had almost been purloined. "I promise to have a hot apple pie with melted cheddar cheese on it waiting for you when you get back, Reb."

The white-haired man grinned and his blue eyes twinkled in the light of two lanterns hanging in the barn. "Sight better promise than J.D. made me to ride with him after Katherine. All he had was Yankee dollars."

"Thank you, Cat. This was thoughtful of you," J.D. said as she poured two cups of coffee.

"It's tasty, too. A man livin' alone forgets just how good a woman's cookin' is," Reb added.

A gentle smile uplifted the corners of Caitlyn's mouth. In spite of her attempt to hide it when she noticed J.D.'s gaze on her, she failed to erase it. Nor could she disguise the warmth in her tone. "It's the least I could do for my man."

"You slipped, Cat." J.D. winked at her and smiled.

She answered with a frown. "Slipped?"

"You said, 'my man,'" he replied. "Does that mean something has changed that you should tell me about?"

"It means that I slipped," she said, the edge that J.D. had noticed yesterday returning to her voice.

J.D. shrugged. "Can't blame a man for wishful thinking."

Before Caitlyn could answer, a ranch hand walked into the barn. "Mr. McQuay, the sun's comin' up. The boys and I are ready to move out when you give the word."

"Might as well get on with it," J.D. replied, following the cowboy outside.

Ten other ranch hands sat astride mounts and surrounded a string of six more pack mules. Each man carried a rifle in hand and a Colt strapped to his hip. The mules carried boxes on their backs, the containers weighted so as to look as if they were carrying gold.

"Good luck, gentlemen, and thanks," J.D. said as the eleven moved southward with the mules. He then turned to Caitlyn. "I don't know if that decoy is going to fool anyone, but it was a damned fine idea of yours."

"It won't hurt," Reb added. "And it just might sidetrack anybody that's been keepin' an eye on the ranch."

J.D. had spoken the truth. Caitlyn's decoy party was a good idea. To draw would-be trouble away from the real shipment of gold, the eleven men would ride southwest toward Presidio for two days and then turn around and return to the ranch. For those two days Reb and J.D. intended to head directly south before angling westward toward the border town. J.D. felt grateful to the men who were undertaking to be decoys; their willingness to run the risk was a mark of their loyalty to the McQuay family.

The sandwiches were finished as well as the coffee when Reb and J.D. walked back into the barn and mounted. A simple wish for good luck and godspeed was all that passed between J.D. and Caitlyn as the two men led the mules and horses from the barn and reined them to the south. General Lee took the lead as they moved out onto open prairie, running fifty feet ahead of the two men.

"Has anyone ever told you that you're a fool, J.D.?" Reb twisted around in the saddle and glanced back. Caitlyn stood watching their departure.

"Quite a few, but most soon regretted it," J.D. replied.

"Well, I might regret it, too, but you're one of the damnedest fools I ever met. That woman back there loves you, and unless I miss my bet you still love her. Why in hell did you run off to New Mexico the way you done?"

"Why in hell don't you mind your own business?" J.D. stared straight ahead. It was not the woman he could not live with, it was her airs.

"Damn!" Reb cursed as he looked back at Caitlyn once more. "I thought we'd get farther than a quarter of a mile before trouble caught up with us."

"What?" J.D. shifted his weight in the saddle and stared over his shoulder.

Twenty riders rode past the Big House and came directly for them. J.D. tugged the Winchester from the saddle holster and cocked the weapon. "So much for the decoy!"

The moment he shouldered the rifle, he lowered it. The two riders coming into focus at the lead of the party were Els Brewster and his son, Harlan. J.D. signaled Reb to put away his own weapon. The older man did so with a frustrated grunt.

Throwing up a hand for the men riding with him to halt, Els rode up beside J.D. before reining his own mount to a stop. "I had a feeling you'd try somethin' like this. It's lucky I caught up with you."

"If you're offering to ride with Reb and me, I'm afraid I'll have to turn down the offer," J.D. said. "The last thing I want is to trot into Presidio beside a man wearing a badge."

"I don't think you'll be needin' to make that ride to

the border." Els grinned when J.D.'s brow furrowed with uncertainty. "Them two rangers you was so all fired up about last night have sighted the men who have Katherine."

J.D.'s expression remained unchanged.

"The rangers were riding into town late last night when they caught sight of them coming out of the Del Nortes. A rancher was sent into town to fetch us. The men who have Katherine are about fifteen miles south of here. I want you to ride with *us*. Forget the gold and let's go and get Katherine."

"And I want you and your rangers to back away." There was a knife's edge to the sharpness of J.D.'s tone. "That's my daughter those seven men have, and I don't want her getting hurt in a shoot-out caused by a bunch of men out to make a name for themselves."

Els looked blankly at his old friend. "I don't believe I understand you, J.D."

"Then let me put it plain and simple. I want you to take all those men, except one, back to town. That one man I want you to send to those rangers and tell them to pull back and forget the men holding my daughter. I want this meddling in my affairs to stop. I already told you last night that I intend to play this hand the way it was dealt to me, and I don't need or want any help from the law." He could not think of any way to make it plainer than that.

Els shook his head. "I can't do that, J.D., and you know it. I'm the duly sworn sheriff of Presidio County, and it's my duty to protect her citizens, whether you want it or not. Is that plain and simple enough for you?"

"If that's the way you want it, then that's the way you'll do it. But, Els, there's one more thing." J.D.'s voice grew louder to make certain every man in the posse heard him. "If Katherine suffers any harm because of this, I promise I'll hunt down each and every one of you and kill you."

Harlan nudged his horse forward. "You can't threaten a peace officer like that."

"He ain't makin' a threat, son." Reb's gaze lifted to the young lawman. "He's statin' a fact. If I was you, I'd listen to him."

"J.D., the years have turned you into a stubborn old

fool." Els yanked his horse's head around. "Come on, boys, we've got a job to do."

His eyes narrowed to slits and his mouth drawn in a tight line, J.D. watched the twenty men ride on defiantly ahead of him. He nudged his own horse forward at a steady, even walk. He had just sworn to kill twenty men. He prayed to God that he would never have reason to make good his word.

Chapter Eight

Anywhere else the barrier of rock that thrust out of the prairie would be called just hills. In Texas, where highlands were rare, the wall of rock that rose five hundred feet from its base to its jagged granite crests and stretched twenty miles from east to west was a mountain range.

Billy Crow once again proved his worth as a member of Tate Lansdale's seven-man gang when they reached the mountains, as the purples and grays of the predawn sky washed away the nighttime blackness of the eastern horizon. Taking the lead, the half-breed Apache directed his companions to a hundred-foot-wide pass that opened through the five miles of rugged, lichen-spotted, wind-weathered boulders. A mile into the pass, Billy drew his mount up and signaled for the others to halt. He then reined back to Lansdale, who had taken rear guard since leaving the Del Norte Mountains.

"The sun will soon be up. There is a place to camp among the rocks here."

Lansdale's gaze followed the tilt of the Indian's head to the right. He saw nothing but a sheer wall of granite with shattered boulders, three times the size of a man, strewn like talus at its base. "I don't see anythin'."

The hair on the back of Lansdale's neck bristled. For the thousandth time since beginning the night's ride, he studied the terrain and narrow horizon in the pass behind him. And for the thousandth time he saw nothing. He cursed silently. Maybe he was just overreacting, but since Dwayne Holt had brought word of the Texas Rangers' being on their tail, he had been unable to shake the sensation that unseen eyes were burning into the back of his head.

Billy pointed to a trio of elongated boulders that rested on end, leaning against each other as though for mutual support. "They are called the Old Men by my people. Behind them is a narrow path that leads to a cave. It is large enough for all of us and our horses." He turned to Lansdale. "The way to the south is open grassland for half a day's ride. Today we will find no better place to hide."

Lansdale had not considered stopping this soon. He wanted to put as much distance between the Del Nortes and himself as possible. However, the alternative—the possibility of being discovered while exposed and defenseless on the open range—sat none too well with him. His original plan was to lay up during the day and make the ride for Presidio under the cover of night.

"Tate, we gonna ride or camp and get some rest?" Holt called to him. "We ain't gettin' nowhere just sittin' here."

Ignoring Holt's attempt to rile him, Lansdale took another glance over his shoulder and then studied the rocks ahead again. He knew the original plan to travel only at night was a good one. He would stick to it. He nodded to Billy. "We'll give this cave of yours a try."

Billy eased his mount around and rode behind the Old Men with the other outlaws following in single file. To climb the five hundred feet to the promised cave, they wove back and forth along a narrow switchback path that twisted through boulders and past eroded pillars of granite. By now the early morning sun was beginning to warm the stone walls in a red glow, but the men still inched forward in the chilly sweat that came automatically with the fear of discovery.

The cave to which Billy led them was no more than a half-domed recess in the mountain formed when a portion of the rock face had collapsed. It was, however, as Billy had said, large enough to hide the seven men and their single captive.

While the others tended their mounts and the two pack mules or spread out their bedrolls, Lansdale left

Katherine McQuay under Ray Powell's watchful eye, took two twists of beef jerky from a sack Kelly Carter passed around, and walked farther up the mountain along a foot-worn path that led away from the cave.

As weary as a night without sleep had left him, the nagging sensation that someone or something had watched their every move would not let him rest until he was certain of their safety. Reaching the top of the rocky ridge, he picked his way northward. The elevation of this lofty vantage point would give him an unhampered view of the plains all the way back to Monte Verde.

Halfway back toward the beginning of the pass, the sharp crack of one rock striking another froze him in his tracks. His eyes darted from side to side, but saw nothing unusual. The sound came again; this time he located it and the crush of gravel beneath boots that followed. They came from below, in the pass itself.

Cautiously Lansdale picked his way among the boulders until he could peer down. His heart pounded as he caught his breath. Two men were below, the same ones he had seen searching the Del Nortes yesterday—the two rangers whom the Monte Verde sheriff had called in to track them.

"Damn!" Lansdale cursed softly as he watched one of the rangers scramble back down the rock face of the pass and swing into the saddle of a horse his mounted companion held waiting for him. How had the two lawmen followed them throughout the night and gone completely unnoticed? How had he missed them? The two must be real experts, Tate grumbled to himself—not as easily fooled as that two-bit sheriff and his son back in Monte Verde.

Inching closer to the edge of the rock face, Lansdale strained to hear as the rangers spoke. Their voices rose to him as little more than a whisper on the morning air, but he could hear.

"You read 'em right, Clay. They're holed up in that old Indian cave where we ran down Bill Hitt and his brother two years ago. It won't be hard to—"

A gust of wind momentarily ripped the words away.

"—when the others get here."

Others? Lansdale's head jerked around, and he peered to the north. His throat went dry and cotton filled his mouth. A column of dust out on the prairie confirmed what he had just overheard. Riders were moving toward the mountain. How many, he could only guess. The dust rose from a distance of at least ten miles. Two hours, maybe more, remained before the riders reached the pass. *Maybe less!* His mind raced, trying desperately to find reason amid the panicked spin of his thoughts.

"Let's pull back to the mouth of the pass and wait for Brewster and his posse to get here," one of the rangers' voices drifted up.

"Yeah, no need gettin' too close and givin' ourselves away till we're ready to move in."

The lawmen reined their mounts around and moved out toward the mouth of the narrow pass.

Lansdale stepped back and swallowed hard. He forced himself to remain calm. But when he lifted his hat to smooth his thick black hair, big beads of sweat trickled down his temples. There was time to get ready for that posse. He had come prepared for something like this, although he had not expected the trouble to come so soon, while they were still in the Del Norte Mountains.

Turning, he picked his way back to the cave. His men, all except Ray, who sat guard on the girl, were stretched out in their sleeping blankets.

"Up! All you bastards get on your feet. We've got company." The toes of his boots, applied to rumps and sides, emphasized the urgency of his words.

As the men scrambled to their feet, he quickly explained what he had seen and heard. Hank Yoakum was the first to shake off his daze and ask, "What you got in mind?"

"Hank, I want you and Ray to mount up and take the girl on down to Goat Mountain as fast as you can. The rest of us will catch up with you there tonight." Lansdale did not like being separated from his ticket to half a million in ransom, but unless he arranged a welcome for the rangers and the posse, he would have no chance of getting the money in the first place.

While Hank and Ray did as ordered, Lansdale walked to one of the mules. Opening its pack, he pulled out a small keg. The words BLASTING POWDER were stenciled in black paint on the keg's side. He placed it on the ground and grinned at his men. "Soon as I get the other keg out, we'll arrange us a little surprise for them damned meddlin' rangers."

"They're up there among the rocks in an old Lipan Apache cave," Texas Ranger Clay Morgan explained as Els Brewster and the men who rode with him dismounted. "We've got to ride about a mile into the pass to get at them, but there's safe enough ways to do it. Jim and I took two rustlers out of the cave two years back with no problem at all."

"The only trouble I can see," the other ranger said, glancing over the twenty men who had ridden from Monte Verde, "is getting this many men in close without makin' any noise. We didn't expect you to bring along more'n a half dozen men."

Els stiffened at the disapproval he detected in the ranger's voice. After J.D.'s unexpected reaction, the last thing he wanted was a fellow law officer chewing a piece out of his backside. After all, this was his county. "These men are all friends of the McQuay family and have requested to be here. All of them have been duly deputized."

The words were not what he wanted to say, nor was his voice as firm as he wished. He winced inwardly when he noticed the scornful glance that passed between the two rangers. From their expressions it was clear they thought he had made a mistake, but one that they would have to live with.

"Shouldn't we wait and move in after it gets dark?" Harlan stepped beside his father. "There'd be less chance of being noticed then."

Clay Morgan shook his head. "Those men went up into the rocks for a good reason—to sleep. They rode all night and odds are they plan to ride again as soon as the sun sets. The time to make our move is while they're all sawing logs and thinking that they're safe."

His fellow ranger nodded his agreement. "What we'll do is ride in real quiet-like for three-quarters of a mile, dismount and move in on foot. These rocks are riddled with deer paths and old Apache foot trails. If we stay quiet, we can probably get the whole bunch of us up to the cave without being noticed."

Els winced inwardly again. He had no doubt the ranger's last remark had been directed at him. He glanced about; only Harlan seemed to notice the ranger's comment. "When do we move in?"

Morgan squinted overhead at a sun that played hide-and-seek behind the gathering clouds. "Now's as good a time as any, I reckon. Odds are that the men up there have all had themselves a feed and they're stretched out and snoring."

Pursing his lips thoughtfully, Els nodded. "Then let's get on with this. The sooner we get that girl back, the sooner her family can rest easy." *And the sooner Mr. J.D. McQuay will eat crow*, he thought. "Mount up, boys, and keep it quiet. If I hear so much as a cough out of one of you, I'll have your hide to nail on the jailhouse door."

No word passed among the twenty-two men returning to their saddles. Only the crunch of sand and stone beneath hooves and the occasional creak of saddle leather accompanied them as they entered the pass.

His belly flat on top of a granite boulder high on the wall of the pass, Tate Lansdale saw the small army of men before he heard them.

Similarly hidden on the opposite side of the pass, Todd Carter pushed to his knees, lifted his right arm, and waved.

Lansdale returned the signal and watched Todd slide back to disappear from sight. With a quick glance to make certain the rangers and the posse were still approaching through the pass, Lansdale wiggled back and jumped from the boulder.

Billy Crow waited with a smoking stogie in one hand and the end of a fuse in the other. The half-breed tilted his head to the right.

Lansdale's gaze followed the motion, tracing the fuse from Billy's hand and along the ground to where it vanished into a large crevice between two boulders.

"I lodged the powder down deep the way you said."

Billy handed both cigar and fuse to Lansdale. "Once you light that, you have thirty seconds to get clear."

Before Lansdale could question the Indian, Billy had pivoted and trotted back along the path to take cover with Dwayne Holt fifty yards away. Lansdale stuck the cigar between his teeth, clamped down, and waited.

In spite of J.D. and in spite of the rangers' reaction to the posse's size, Els Brewster felt good. The rangers sounded confident. That boosted Els's own belief in what they were about to attempt.

As much as he hated to admit it to himself, Els needed this, needed it badly. After the two men who had robbed the Marathon bank eighteen months ago managed to elude his six-man posse down in the Chinati Mountains, rumors began to spread about the Republicans looking for a candidate to run against him in the fall election.

That had not bothered him; the Republicans were always looking for candidates. The trouble was, they had found one—rancher and former Texas Ranger Ben Ray Vaughan. Though Vaughan had yet to announce, he was making all the noises and moves of a man ready to toss his hat into the ring at the slightest provocation.

If Els rode back into Monte Verde with Katherine McQuay safe again at his side, he'd give the Republicans and Ben Ray Vaughan something to think about. Taking a couple of the kidnappers alive, Els figured, would be a nice finishing touch. A good trial with lots of publicity never hurt a man's chances when the polls finally opened.

A wave of disgust washed over Els. He found it difficult to accept that those thoughts belonged to him. They were not the reflections of a lawman, but of a politician. Somewhere along the line, that's what he had become. Where? He still wore a sheriff's badge on his vest, but upholding the law had taken second place to assuring that he kept a hold on the office. When?

Once, when this portion of the state began to open up, no one wanted the badge he wore. The job was too dangerous. There were a thousand and one ways for a man to die trying to bring law and order to a young land, be it Comanches or Mexican raiders who crossed the Rio Grande to strike the cattle herds. Now, after he had fought long and hard to bring civilization to the Big Bend region, a lot of men were getting the idea that his badge would look good pinned to their own chests.

If he did lose the badge, what would he do then? Els was concerned about more than giving up the status and prestige of being sheriff in Texas's largest county: He was worried about his livelihood. Being a lawman was all he had ever really known. Except for the years during the war when he had donned the Confederate gray, his whole adult life had been spent as a lawman. He was not like Harlan, who was preparing for the inevitable with a small ranch and a few head of cattle. Els had not been that smart; the badge was all he had. He had never considered a time when it might not be his.

Given a few more years, Els thought, he could follow his son's example and start to build something else for himself. But he needed to have those years first or he would—

A blur of motion out of the corner of his eye jerked Els's head to the left. He stared high along the granite wall of the pass. He swore he had seen something up there among the rocks, but there was nothing. Maybe he was more nervous about this than he realized.

Clay Morgan, who rode a few feet ahead of Els, held an arm high to signal a halt. Drawing up his mount, Els stepped from the saddle. Morgan looked back at him and waved him forward.

"Pick a couple of your boys to stay here with the horses," the ranger said. "The rest of us will move on up ahead."

Els nodded his head and then turned back to the posse. Pointing to rancher Tom Ferris and his top wrangler, Chad Robinson, he signaled the two men to gather the reins of the others' horses and await their return.

"Let's move out," Morgan said in a voice no more than a forced whisper.

A roar like the blast of a hundred thunderstorms rent the silence and then shredded it. The ground vibrated, rippled as though it had suddenly come to life and was intent on shaking off any who foolishly trod its surface.

Els's head snapped up. Fragments of shattered rock hurled out from the walls of the pass, preceding a billowing cloud of sand and dust. In a single pounding beat of his heart, he knew what had happened. The kidnappers they had hoped to surprise had sighted their approach and greeted the posse with a surprise of their own—blasting powder!

"Back!" Els shouted as he spun about and darted for the far wall of the pass. "Get out of here! Run!"

No further warning was needed. Twenty-one men turned tail and ran, fleeing the avalanche of broken boulders that collapsed from the rock walls in the narrowest section of the pass.

The second explosion rocked the pass as the posse dashed for a shelter that did not exist.

Again Els's head jerked up to see another blast rip the opposite wall of the pass. He shouted no warning this time, nor did anyone else. There was no need; there was no place to run. The men they had sought to trap had closed a trap of their own, burying the posse under two tumbling walls of rock.

Directly ahead of him, Els saw the boulders, both larger than five men. One lay flat on the ground. The other had fallen atop the first and rested at a forty-five-degree angle to the ground. Beneath the second was open space. No more than a burrow into which a coyote might crawl to escape a sudden downburst of rain, it nonetheless offered the only possible avenue of escape.

Taking two quick strides forward, Els launched himself through the air and dived headfirst beneath the boulder. He groaned as he slammed into the ground, the air driven from his lungs.

The sound of his own distress was lost in the next instant as tons of rock hailed downward, grinding against the granite roof that protected him. Mingled in that roar were screams—of men and horses.

With arms locked over his head, he lay there. How long, he had no idea. The passage of time lost all meaning for him. All he knew were the falling rocks that pounded the earth about him, the dust and sand that filled the air and clogged his mouth and nostrils, and the reverberating hammer of his own heart.

Nor was Els certain when the last of the stones from the walls fell. Beneath him the earth gradually stopped its quaking. The choking dust outside receded and began to settle. He cautiously unfolded his arms from his head and opened his eyes.

Darkness surrounded him. *No,* his head shook, not total darkness. Tiny shafts of murky light penetrated the cloud of dust that still filled the cramped hole. He twisted as best he could to stare behind him. Rocks now blocked the entrance to his shelter.

Thrusting aside thoughts of being buried alive, he scooted backwards until his boots rested solidly against the barrier. With all the strength he could muster, he kicked out. Nothing. He closed his eyes, said a prayer, and tried again.

The barricade of stone gave way. Rock clacked against rock as the barrier collapsed. Light flooded Els's hiding place.

A quavering sigh of relief gusted from Els's lips. His prayers had been answered. Squirming backwards, he wiggled into the daylight and stood.

The pass as they first had seen it was no longer. In its stead lay a heap of jumbled talus piled from one granite face to the other. The roar that had momentarily deafened his ears was gone, replaced by an eerie silence.

"Harlan?" Els called out. There was no answer. Had he been the only one to survive? "Harlan?"

"Pa, over here." To Els's right, near the edge of the shattered rock, his son stood.

"You're all right?" Els was not sure whether to believe his own eyes.

"I'm all right." Harlan's whole body appeared to sag as he spoke. "But Ted Moore isn't. Both his legs are broken. And Gill Hart's dead."

While Els picked his way over the rock to his son's side, eight other men stood to announce that they had miraculously managed to survive the blasts. Six, including the two rangers, had not. The remaining six men lay injured, arms and legs crushed by the falling granite.

"We've got to try and find what horses we can." In spite of the shocked daze in his eyes, Harlan spoke. "Ted here will die unless we can get him some help."

Els nodded and turned to his left. Ten of the horses had not escaped the avalanche. Their twisted, bloodied bodies lay half buried beneath the rock. The other mounts—he could only guess where they had scattered. It could take hours to find the animals, if they had not fled in total panic all the way back to Monte Verde.

"I'll get a couple of men to go after the horses," Els answered. "Meanwhile, we'll do what we can for Ted and the others."

When Els turned, the bark of a rifle report came from high above and echoed off the walls of granite. Jeb Livingston, a Monte Verde merchant, cried out. His body jerked and twisted as a crimson flower blossomed on his chest.

Two more rifle shots came from the men hidden in the rocks above before Els could free the pistol holstered on his hip. He thumbed back the hammer and lifted the Colt to return the fire.

His finger never even squeezed around the trigger. An unseen hammer slammed between his shoulder blades and hurled him forward. He stumbled, trying to maintain his footing on the jumble of rocks and failing. He collapsed face down on the ground. Try as he did, he could not make his body rise again. All that he could do was lie there as blackness rose about him and sucked him into its unfathomable depths.

Chapter Nine

Saddle leather creaked beneath J.D.'s weight as he shifted in the saddle and gazed over his shoulder. He scanned the lush green prairie from horizon to horizon. The only moving creatures within sight were grazing pronghorns to the east.

That he saw nothing but the antelopes did not lessen the disquieting sensation that he and Reb were being followed. Five hundred thousand in gold was enough to make a full platoon of soldiers nervous, he told himself, but that did not help. J.D. was certain some fool would try to relieve them of their precious burden. It was just a matter of when. The moment they had ridden away from the Circle Q, they had become an open target.

Shifting forward again, he scanned the terrain ahead of them. Open range ran for miles to the south, ending in a line of jagged-crested mountains. It was there Els had taken his posse to meet the rangers. J.D. tried to edge from his mind the abductors and what they would attempt, but he could not. Katherine might be captive in those hills, and she was as vulnerable to a stray bullet as were the seven men who had kidnapped her.

"You better settle down, man. You're actin' as fidgety as a young girl out on her first moonlight buggy ride." Reb hiked a questioning eyebrow at his companion. "What's got into you?"

J.D. jerked a thumb over his shoulder. "It isn't in me. It's what those mules are carrying. I've got the damnedest feeling that Caitlyn's decoy isn't working and that we have company shadowing us."

Reb stood in the stirrups and twisted to the left and then the right. "Don't see nothin'." He settled back into the saddle. "I think it's what's happenin' up yonder that's eatin' at you."

"Could be." J.D. shrugged. "But something's worrying the General too. He's been running to and fro, dodging in and out, ever since we got started."

Reb squinted ahead, studying the dog that ran before them. J.D. was right. General Lee darted far to one side and then dashed off in the opposite direction. His muzzle dipped to sniff the ground and then his head jerked up, ears twitching this way and that.

"This is new territory to him," Reb said. "He's just givin' it a good checkin' out. Or maybe he's lookin' for a rabbit."

J.D. shrugged again. Neither of Reb's explanations for General Lee's unusual activity was satisfactory. The dog sensed something in the air, and it was the identity of that something that troubled J.D.

Reaching back, Reb patted a saddlebag. "In here I've got that old spyglass I used when I was scoutin' for the army. Would it make you feel better if you took a gander through it?"

J.D. considered the small telescope for a moment and then waved away the offer. Grasslands were treacherously deceptive. To the eye, even with the aid of a spyglass, the prairie appeared to be a flat, featureless plain. It was anything but that. It rolled gently, and occasionally swelled to hilly knolls. Then there were creek beds that cut through the land—eroded trenches that could hide mounted men as easily as hills.

"Looks to be water up ahead." Reb pointed to the south. "Think we should give the stock a rest?"

"Might as well."

J.D. sighted the water hole. The morning sun glinted off a small pool no more than a few feet in diameter. This could be a puddle left by the rains. Or it could come from some underground source. Occasionally, during the summer, water seeped to the surface to fill depressions in the ground, forming water holes that vanished overnight. It was the minerals such groundwater contained that concerned the men of this country. Too much salt and alkaline, and the water could kill.

Reaching the shallow pool, J.D. dismounted and knelt beside it. He dipped a cupped palm into the muddy water. As he pulled his hand out, he leaned over, puckered his lips, and sucked a sampling into his mouth. He tentatively swished the gritty water from cheek to cheek for several seconds, checking for a brackish flavor.

"Well," Reb demanded, "is it good?"

Swallowing, J.D. nodded. "As sweet as a man's likely to find at this time of year."

The old Indian scout grunted as he stepped from the saddle and knelt on one knee beside the water hole. "It seems I recollect trustin' you with the water once up near Horsehead Crossing—much to my regret. I'd best make my own judgment of the quality of this here water."

"You're never going to let me forget that copperas creek, are you?" J.D. smiled and shook his head while watching his friend taste the water. "That was almost twenty years ago, if you'll think on it a moment. I was still a mite wet behind the the ears then."

Reb wiped his mouth on a shirtsleeve. "Me and about a score of men ain't never goin' to forget that night, or are any of us likely to let you forget about it. You kept us all hoppin' that night. You was damned lucky one of us didn't kill you for that dumb stunt—or leave you all staked out for the first Comanche that come along. Copperas water— never seen a growed man that didn't know copperas water."

J.D. smiled again as he took another palmful of water from the muddy hole. Nearly two decades ago, shortly after coming to Monte Verde, he had ridden north along the Pecos River after a Comanche raiding party with a group of more seasoned Indian fighters. Being the youngest of the men, he had drawn cooking duty. One evening while the others tended the mounts, he had drawn water from a nearby creek and prepared catch-as-catch-can stew from two jackrabbits and an armadillo that had been shot during the day.

The meal, as he recalled, had been quite a success, drawing praise from the older men—until an hour after supper. That was when the moaning and groaning began, and the men started hugging their cramping bellies and hastening off to the privacy of the broombrush.

J.D. had never heard of copperas until that day, but the mineral and its taste was something he had never forgotten since. As many of the men colorfully told him the next morning, the creek from which he had drawn water for the stew was rich in the natural purgative.

Eventually, he lived down that incident and it was forgotten by the others he had ridden with. All except Reb, who seemed to take delight in dredging up memories of that night on every possible occasion, especially when it would afford J.D. the greatest embarrassment.

"You know, you old mountain goat, I would've thought twice about hiring you to ride with me if I had remembered how much pleasure you took in bringing up that copperas stew." J.D. stood and led his horse and mules to the water. "Did it ever occur to you that I might have used that water on purpose to get out of doing all the cooking?"

"It occurred to me." Reb's head cocked to one side and he winked at his friend. "But the way I reflected on it was you just didn't have the smarts to go and pull somethin' that stupid on purpose."

J.D. had to turn his back to hide a smile when Reb began to chuckle with decided relish. Like most minor disasters in a man's life, time seems to grind away the painful edges, leaving everything wrapped in a soft cloth of humor. As seen from a distance of twenty years, that night was funny. He had never seen twenty men move so quickly or so often.

Once again the niggling sensation that they were being followed crept into his mind. His gaze swept over the prairie. Still there was nothing.

"Reb, see to watering the stock. I'm going to borrow that spyglass of yours and go up yonder and take a look-see." He tilted his head toward a small hill about an eighth of a mile to the west.

Untying the flap to a saddlebag, Reb dug out the small brass telescope and passed it to his friend. J.D. nodded his thanks and then quickly strode to the crest of the rise. He opened the spyglass to the full extension of its

three sections and lifted the eyepiece to his right eye.
Meticulously he scanned from east to west and then
retraced his action. Nothing, there was nothing to be
seen.

He then turned and pointed the telescope at the
mountains to the south. Nothing in that direction, either.

He slapped the instrument closed in what should
have been a satisfying move but was not. Walking back to
the water hole, he spoke to Reb. "Couldn't see a thing."

Reb's head bobbed in acceptance, as though that was
exactly what he had expected. He took the telescope from
J.D. and returned it to the saddlebag, coming out with a
leather pouch from which he extracted a strip of jerked
beef that he stuck in the corner of his mouth like a cigar.
"Want some?"

J.D. accepted a strip and then broke it in two, tossing
half of the dried, peppery meat to General Lee, who came
bounding up.

"You never got around to answerin' me earlier," Reb
said.

"About what?" J.D.'s brow furrowed.

"'Bout you and Caitlyn," Reb replied. "If I recall
correctly, I was askin' why you two went and busted up
the way you did."

"We're still married." J.D.'s words came in a terse,
sharp gust.

"On a piece of paper maybe." Reb ignored his friend's
obvious dislike of broaching the subject of his separation.
"But it ain't no marriage when a man and wife live with
half a country separatin' them."

"It's the one marriage I have." J.D. turned and stared
coldly at Reb. "Didn't I mention that this was none of your
business? If I didn't, let me say it now—my marriage is
none of your goldarn business."

Reb's mouth twisted to one side. He shook his head
and spat. "One of the advantages of gettin' to be an old
man is the right to go stickin' your nose into places it don't
belong."

"You run the risk of getting that nose punched," J.D.
warned.

"Wouldn't be the first time," Reb continued. "The older a man gets, J.D.—"

"Don't give me that line about getting wiser," J.D. tried to head off his friend. "You've never had a wise bone in your body."

"—the more he starts seein' this world in a different light." Undaunted, Reb totally ignored the remark. "Maybe 'cause he's knowin' he ain't got all the time he once had, he gets to cuttin' through all the bull manure people heap 'round themselves to hide the real reason they go about doin' the things they do. It gets down to the fact a man just ain't got that much time to waste to go spendin' it on double-talk and crap."

J.D. eyed his friend. "Speaking of double-talk, why don't you just come out and say what you're trying to get at?"

"All right." Reb's chest inflated. "You ain't that old, and you oughtta believe a man who has a few years on you, J.D. You still have half a lifetime ahead of you. Why don't you stop actin' like such a dang-blasted fool and get back together with Caitlyn? That's where you belong. Never in my life did I ever see two people that were meant to be together more than you and Caitlyn."

"That was before she started with her airs," J.D. answered.

"'Airs'? Dammit, J.D., three years 'fore you lit off for New Mexico, you was always mumblin' about Caitlyn's 'airs.' Just what in hell do you mean by that word?"

J.D.'s eyes narrowed. "What do you mean, what do I mean? Just look at the Big House and all those guests she's always having. And those parties and—"

"Seems to me, she might go a tad bit overboard now and then," Reb cut him off, "but I always thought she kinda earned the right to all that. As I remember it, it weren't just one Jonathan David McQuay that built the Circle Q into what it is."

J.D.'s eyes went wide. He had not realized until that moment that Reb knew his full name.

"Seems I recollect a certain woman workin' right alongside her husband, scratchin' to make somethin' out of what most folks would have seen as nothin' in the first place."

"You don't know what you're talking about." J.D. shook his head. "You don't understand the way it is."

Reb shrugged. "Maybe not, but from where I stand, both of you look to be spoiled children in bad need of bein' thrown over a knee and havin' your tails tanned."

The mental image Reb's words invoked brought a chuckle from J.D.'s throat. "And who in all of Presidio County has the courage to try and turn Caitlyn Marie Kennedy McQuay over his knee?"

The question gave Reb pause. His chest deflated, and his shoulders sagged. "Reckon you've got a point there. Tanglin' with Caitlyn would be like tryin' to take on two or five mountain lions—"

"With a couple of bobcats and rattlesnakes thrown in," J.D. added. "Believe me, I've butted heads with that woman on more than one occasion. There is no way that a natural-born man can expect to come out a winner."

Reb edged back his hat and scratched his head. "Maybe that's part of the problem? Both of you are tryin' to win when there ain't nothin' to win."

J.D.'s mouth opened, but he had no answer. There was something in what his friend said that struck closer to home than he wanted to admit.

"What's the matter? Cat suddenly got your tongue?" Reb pressed.

"Old man, you're pushing at something that's best left—"

The rumble of distant thunder left J.D.'s sentence hanging in the air, unfinished. Both he and Reb looked up to a sky dotted with fluffy patches of white.

"It don't look like no rain to me." Reb's forehead knitted.

J.D. pointed to a line of clouds just above the south-western horizon. "Might be some showers moving in from that direction."

A second roll of thunder rumbled through the air.

"Seems like them clouds are awful far away to be hearin' thunder, but this country can play tricks with sounds sometimes." Reb tugged his hat firmly down on his head. "Ain't nothin' worse than ridin' in the rain. Leaves a man feelin' as bad on the inside as he feels on the outside."

J.D. nodded his agreement. "There's an old cave the Lipans used to use up in those mountains ahead. If a storm catches us, we can camp there for the night."

Reb glanced to the north as he mounted. His eyes searched from horizon to horizon. "If I remember that cave rightly, it's a good spot to defend against unwanted visitors."

J.D. watched his friend for a moment. Reb had caught a case of the fidgets from him. The old Indian scout was not looking over his shoulder to enjoy the view behind them. He too was searching now for those "uninvited visitors."

"What are you waiting for?" Reb's head turned to him. "It ain't Saturday night, and I got no desire to take a bath if we can help it."

J.D. swung into the saddle and moved forward, leading a string of five mules and one horse behind him. Once again General Lee ran ahead, scouting the path before them.

Chapter Ten

Harlan Brewster cautiously poked his head above the boulder he lay behind. His hazel eyes carefully scanned the face of the granite wall to his right and then jumped to the rock face to his left. He saw nothing, but that meant little. Other than the puffs of smoke floating from the rocks up high in the pass, he had never even seen the gunmen who had cut down his father and the others.

"Jeff?" Harlan called out. "Eddy? You two still there?"

"I ain't goin' nowheres," Jeff Clapton shouted back. "I'm stickin' right here till you tell me otherwise."

"I'm here," Eddy Martin answered. "But Hal ain't. He's dead, Harlan. Died on me about a half hour ago. His eyes just rolled back in his head and he stopped breathin'."

Harlan closed his eyes and silently mouthed a curse. He wished it could have been a prayer. Out of the twenty-two men who had ridden into the pass, Eddy, Jeff, and he were the only ones capable now of standing and fighting. There were at least three others alive. He heard their moans, but his calls for them to identify themselves went unanswered. He assumed they were unconscious or delirious from the agony of their wounds. Either way, they could not be counted on.

"Harlan," Jeff shouted. "You think they're still up there waitin' for us to show ourselves?"

"I don't know." Harlan swallowed hard, his gaze again scouring the rock faces that rose around him. The shadows and the crevices between the boulders could easily hide an army of desperadoes.

"It's been an hour, maybe more, since they stopped shootin'," Eddy said. "They could've pulled out by now."

Harlan slipped a pocket watch from his vest and opened it with a thumb. An hour and a half had indeed passed since the outlaws above had poured a volley into the rock-strewn pass. They had waited only thirty minutes between their first attack and the second.

Jeff spoke again. "I think Eddy's right. They ain't up there no more. But I ain't standin' up and makin' myself a target just to prove a point."

Harlan's gaze skimmed over the mounds of rock clogging the pass. Fifty feet from his position, his father's body lay motionless atop a jagged boulder half the size of a man. With Els and the rangers dead, he was now in command. There might be only two men to command, but the duty still rested on his shoulders, whether he wanted it or not.

Summoning all the courage he could find within him, he called out. "I'm going to stand."

Before either of the men answered, Harlan stood up in full view.

The barking reports of rifles he expected did not come. Silence filled the pass. He faced the right wall and then the left. No one fired on his exposed body. A relieved sigh hissed from between his lips. *Lord, help us get out of here.*

"They're gone," he called to the others as confidently as he could. "They've pulled out. They're gone."

Gradually, still uncertain of Harlan's pronouncement, Jeff and Eddy pushed from behind the boulders that had sheltered them. With eyes wide they stared about. The tension in their bodies slowly lessened as they accepted the fact that the gunmen had probably abandoned the rocks above.

"They're gone," Harlan repeated.

Both men turned and faced him.

"We've work to do," he said. "First we have to sort the living from the dead, then find a way to get the injured back to Monte Verde."

Neither Eddy nor Jeff answered. They simply began the grim task assigned to them.

*   *   *

Reb tugged back on the reins, bringing his mount to a dead stop. "My eyes ain't what they once was, but I'll be damned if that don't look like a horse wearin' a saddle over yonder."

"Where?" J.D. halted his own horse and glanced at his companion.

"There." Reb pointed to the east. "That is a saddled horse, ain't it?"

"It is." J.D.'s eyes narrowed.

In the next instant, his head jerked around to the mountains rising a mile to the south. A hundred fears shot through his mind. All of them centered on one thing—the posse and the likely consequences of their raid on Katherine's kidnappers. Able-bodied Texas men did not let saddled horses roam free. Something had gone wrong! He could feel it in his bones.

"Damn!" His bootheels dug into his mount's sides as he clucked the mules behind him to life.

"What in hell's got into you?" Reb stared at his friend.

There was no answer. J.D. urged horse and mules into an easy gallop, then pushed them to a run.

Cursing, Reb did the same.

A quarter of a mile from the entrance to the pass, J.D. sighted three more saddled horses grazing freely. His heart pounded, trying to escape his chest. He realized that if Els and his rangers had already succeeded in pulling off a rescue, they would have met them returning from the mountains with Katherine by now. They had seen nothing but a handful of pronghorns and the four horses.

J.D. entered the pass without hesitation. He covered a half mile before he drew up his mount and stared ahead, dumbfounded, his jaw sagging.

"That weren't no thunder we heard back at the water hole." Reb halted beside his companion. Like J.D. he was stunned at the sight of a barrier of shattered rock that now blocked the pass a quarter of a mile ahead. "That was blastin' powder, sure as my ma named me Jeremy Clancy Boggs."

Reb gave voice to the obvious. J.D. did not need a newspaper account to imagine what had happened. Els, the rangers, and the posse had ridden blindly into the pass and most likely none of them would ever come out. The kidnappers had been ready for them with enough blasting powder to bury an army.

"Somebody's moving over there to the left." Reb jabbed an arm in the air. "Can't believe anybody managed to live through this mess."

Neither could J.D. Not that what he believed mattered at the moment. He nudged his mount forward, tugging the mules after him. Reb followed.

J.D. did not recognize two of the men who turned and faced them as they approached. But the third was Harlan Brewster. The young man's face was drawn and haggard, a reflection of the hell he must have faced and somehow survived right here in this pass during the past couple of hours.

"Mr. McQuay?" Harlan's squinting eyes widened in recognition. His voice was dry and thin. "Mr. McQuay, I had forgotten about you coming up behind us. You don't know how lucky we are that you showed up just now."

J.D.'s eyes surveyed the bodies lined in a neat, funereal row in the sand. Els Brewster was among them. He closed his eyes and said a silent prayer for the departed soul of an old friend.

"It looks like you ran out of luck long before me and J.D. rode up." Reb sadly shook his head in disgust when he saw the dead men. He doffed his round-brimmed hat for a few seconds and looked up to the sky.

"They brought half the mountain down on us." Jeff Clapton stepped forward. "If that wasn't enough, they picked the rest of us off with rifles. We didn't stand a chance."

Harlan looked at J.D. "Jeff there and Eddy and me are the only ones who can still stand. We got four wounded men—badly wounded. The rest are dead. It's like Jeff said, we didn't have a chance."

J.D. said nothing. Robbing the enemy of the opportunity to defend himself was the whole purpose of an ambush. He found it hard to accept that Els, let alone two Texas Rangers, had allowed themselves to walk straight into a trap like this.

"If you'll help us, we can get the wounded and the dead back to town," Harlan continued. "It's getting late in the day. It'll be after dark before we can make it back to Monte Verde as it is."

"Help you?" J.D. stared at the young man in confusion.

"The wounded, Mr. McQuay," Harlan answered, pointing behind him to where the injured men lay. "We have to get them back to town or they'll die."

J.D. pursed his lips and shook his head. "You might have to get those four men back to town, but right now they are of no concern to me."

Harlan blinked; his face went blank. "What do you mean? You have to help us get them into town before they die."

"If you're waiting for me to take them into Monte Verde, then you might as well start digging their graves right here," J.D. answered, his voice hard and cold. "Reb and I have business to attend to in Presidio, not in Monte Verde. My daughter has been kidnapped, in case you've forgotten."

Harlan's gaze turned to the line of dead and then moved back to J.D. He thrust an arm toward the dead men once again. "Those men were your neighbors and friends." Harlan's tone vacillated between accusation and plea. "And in case you've forgotten, they died trying to rescue your daughter, Mr. McQuay!"

J.D. glanced at the ground and shook his head again resolutely before looking back at Els's son. "Don't go trying to place the blame for their dying on either my daughter or me, son. Neither one of us had a thing to do with it. Those men died because of their own actions— actions that went against me and the way I wanted things handled. Your pa and every one of those men heard me good and clear when I asked them to stay out of this. But they went ahead and did as they wanted. I'm sorry they had to pay such a high price for their decisions, but I'm not to be blamed."

"But Mr. McQuay . . ." Harlan's words trailed off in an incoherent sputter as though he were uncertain what to say. Disgust and contempt darkened his features. "My pa always spoke of you as a good man."

"I like to think of myself as such—also practical." J.D. had several harder things to add, but he left them unspoken. The young man had just seen his father murdered and had almost lost his own life. He was confused, and his thinking was out of kilter.

"Then what about the spare horses you got there?" Eddy Martin spoke up. "If you ain't even Christian enough to lend us a hand, let us have them horses and a couple of them mules. Then we can manage all right on our own."

Reb sucked at his teeth in disgust. He glanced at J.D. and pursed his lips. The message was plain: Let these fools clean up a fool's mess.

"I guess I'm not making myself clear," J.D. said. "I've no intention of helping you or giving up any of the stock with me. You men might have caused my daughter grievous injury if you had managed to pull off what you came here to do. Now because of that avalanche"—he pointed to the mass of rock that blocked the pass—"I'll have to ride miles out of my way, costing me valuable time. I'm not about to pay men for throwing up more fences than there already are between my daughter and me."

"Then listen to me, McQuay," Harlan said, his right hand creeping to the pistol on his hip. "If you won't turn the horses and mules over to us willingly, I guess I'm going to have to confiscate them."

The young deputy never had the chance to free revolver from leather. Reb's own pistol pointed directly at Harlan's chest. The hammer was pulled all the way back. "Now who's not actin' very Christianly?"

Harlan's hand pulled away from his sidearm. "Then you're going to just leave us here? And let those men die?"

"I'm afraid that's the way of it." J.D. tugged his mount's head around and started out of the pass.

Behind him, he heard Reb warn, "Don't none of you boys do anythin' stupid, like tryin' to put a chunk of lead in our backs. Believe me, bein' in the shape you're in, a ninety-three-year-old woman with the rheumatism in both her hands could outdraw all three of you."

Reb once more rode at J.D.'s side when he reached the mouth of the pass. J.D. signaled his friend to halt, and looked back down the pass as he pulled his own horse up. "Think I was too hard on that boy, Reb?"

"You spoke the truth plain and simple," Reb answered.

"That's not what I asked you. Was I too hard on him?"

Reb scratched his fingers through his whiskers and looked down at General Lee. "I reckon if Katherine was my daughter, I'd have said everythin' you had to say, and then some."

"I hear an unspoken 'but' in your voice," J.D. said.

"I also reckon I'd have tried to do somethin' for them three. They're up a mighty rocky creek without a paddle or a canoe the way they're standin' right now."

J.D. sucked in a breath through his teeth and exhaled it just as noisily. "Yeah, I see it the same way." He glanced around. "I reckon we aren't going to make that many more miles today anyway, not with the pass being blocked the way it is."

Reb smiled. "We sighted four horses back a piece. Them three will get a damned sight farther with four horses than they will on foot."

"Just what I was thinking." J.D. glanced at his friend. "What do you say to staying here with these mules while I round up those mounts?"

Reb nodded. "I could do with a spell to cool my heels. But I was thinkin' a few of them cedars up that slope would go to makin' a couple of travois to tie the dead and wounded to, for the trip back to town. I know it'd be bumpy as all hell, bein' drug along on a stretcher like that, but there sure ain't no wagon in sight to carry 'em."

J.D. glanced up the mountainside, nodded his assent to Reb's idea, and then handed him his string of mules. "Take the stock back to Harlan to guard. Then you and those other two can go after the cedars."

"Sounds like a good enough plan to me."

As Reb swung his mount around and reentered the pass, J.D. moved out onto the open prairie to find the four stray horses to help save a bunch of reckless cowpokes he still thought were fools.

J.D. returned to the pass leading six stray horses. Reb and the other men stood waiting with four makeshift travois constructed of interwoven cedar branches. No self-respecting Comanche or Apache would ever be caught with such flimsy contraptions, but these travois only had to hold together until they reached Monte Verde.

Dismounting, J.D. helped the others attach the travois to four of the horses' saddles. The improvised triangular stretchers stuck out behind the horses about ten feet, at an angle low to the ground. Two of the wounded men were placed on two of the travois, while the remaining two men were laid out with the dead on the other two travois. Macabre as these arrangements were, they were the best available, and Harlan Brewster knew it.

"Now," J.D. said as he stepped into a stirrup and remounted, "we've been too long from what we have to do. Reb and I can make another five or so miles before the sun sets. When you reach the Circle Q, my wife will outfit you with a buckboard to get you the rest of the way into Monte Verde."

"Mr. McQuay, I ain't going back into town with Jeff and Eddy." Harlan approached J.D. "I'm going to ride with you, if you'll have me and give me loan of one of those spare horses you're leading."

"Son . . ." J.D. started to answer.

But Harlan had not had his say. "If you won't let me ride, then I'll follow along behind you on foot."

Reb's eyes shot to J.D., and his eyebrows arched high, as though silently saying, "What did you expect from one so young?"

"Harlan, now listen to me real good. I tried to explain to you and your pa last night that I was going to handle this my way. That means only Reb and I will ride to Presidio." J.D.'s voice carried a tone of finality. To him the matter was closed. But to make certain the young deputy understood, he added, "Reb and I have ridden together many times in the past. Each of us knows how the other thinks and acts. There isn't room for another man."

Harlan chewed at his lower lip and glanced at the ground for a few moments; then his eyes lifted to J.D. again. "Mr. McQuay, that's my father lying dead over yonder, and those are my friends. If you were in my boots, you wouldn't take no for an answer, nor would you let anyone stand between you and the men who did that. Neither will I." He paused to draw a breath. "I already said it, but I'll say it again. If you won't give me loan of one of them horses, then I'll follow you on foot, 'cause I'm going with you."

"J.D., want I should put a slug in his right foot? He won't be thinkin' about doin' much walkin' then." Reb's voice was devoid of even a hint of humor.

Harlan's hazel eyes shifted to the old Indian fighter. He swallowed when he saw the hard expression on the older man's face; it left no doubt Reb was capable of pulling the trigger of his already drawn and cocked Colt if J.D. just gave him a nod.

J.D. sucked in a steady breath. This boy was pushing, and he was doing his best not to push back. "Son, I'm sorry about what happened to Els, truly I am. He was a friend, and he'll be missed. But this isn't a ride for vengeance, no matter how it may look to you. I'm riding to Presidio for one reason and one reason alone—to save my daughter. I've no need for a man who's out to kill the men who murdered his father."

Harlan sucked in a breath of his own. "I know that, Mr. McQuay. I won't be riding for those men. I've known Katherine all my life, and we've been friends for all that time. I'll be riding to finish what we tried to do here today—to free her."

Reb looked at J.D. "I can still put a bullet in his foot, if you want me to. It'll bring this conversation you're havin' to a right quick halt."

"Put your iron away; there's been enough shooting here today." J.D. looked back at Harlan, studying him for several moments. There was something in his voice when he mentioned Katherine's name that he could not quite put a finger on. "I'm going to say this one more time, Harlan. If you've got some notion about gunning down the men who killed your pa, then point yourself north and head back for Monte Verde, because I've no use for you. But if what you just said is true, and you're willing to take orders—to do exactly what I say, when I say—then I'm willing to give you a try."

"You call all the shots, Mr. McQuay," Harlan answered.

J.D.'s eyes narrowed skeptically, but he had set down the conditions and the young man had accepted them. And there was no denying that an extra man—and his gun—would come in handy. "All right," J. D. said. "But you know my rules, and I expect you to stick to them. If you don't, I'll break you in two with my bare hands—that I promise you."

"That was understood without you saying," Harlan replied.

Nodding to the mules he led, J.D. said, "There's a saddled filly tied behind these mules. If you can find yourself a rifle that works among all those rocks, get it and mount up. There's still some riding I want to put under me before the sun goes down."

"Yes, sir—and thank you, sir. My own Winchester is still over yonder where I was pinned down, but I don't have any ammunition for it."

"We've cartridges enough to spare for you on the pack mule. Now get your rifle and get mounted on the filly." J.D. watched Harlan hasten to the rocks to retrieve his rifle.

"I don't know about this, J.D." Reb turned to his friend and spat thoughtfully at the ground between them. "If you ask me, it would'a been a lot easier to shoot his foot than havin' to wet-nurse him all the way to Presidio."

"Nobody asked you" was all that J.D. answered. But he could not help but wonder if Reb might be right.

Chapter Eleven

A narrow stream that trickled from the mountains fed the rock-bottomed, crystal-clear pool. Others less knowledgeable of the region might have set their camp beside the abundant water. J.D. ordered the two men with him to stop, water the stock, and recheck canteens and water bags. When that was accomplished, he pointed to a semicircle of boulders standing at the base of a mountain a quarter of a mile to the south. There he ordered that camp be made for the coming night. The water hole offered too many dangers from night predators such as cougars and wolves that might slip down from the rocks to prey on animals—men included—that came to drink from the pool.

"Cold camp or fire?" Reb asked when they reached J.D.'s chosen spot.

"Campfire, if we can find enough wood or chips." J.D. dismounted and loosened his saddle's cinch.

Common sense told him that he should follow the old Texas Ranger tradition of leaving horses saddled and ready to ride throughout the night should the need arise. Common sense also told him that the mules needed to be unloaded and given a full rest until morning. Gold was a mighty heavy burden for their small, sinewy backs, and they had to make it all the way to Presidio. He pulled the saddle from his mount and ordered the packs unloaded from the mules.

"If we're going to have a fire, I noticed some pronghorns about a half mile to the west," Harlan said. "If you're not opposed to fresh meat for supper, I can ride out and see if I can bring one down."

J.D. nodded the go-ahead and watched the young man ride off with General Lee trotting behind him. When he turned back to Reb, he found his friend scanning the north. "Still feel someone's tailing us?"

"Strong as you had it earlier." Reb scratched at the whiskers covering his chin. "I got a mind to backtrack a mite and take a look-see. It's gettin' dark enough so as I won't be noticed."

"I can handle the fire and watch the stock," J.D. answered. "Take that gelding you've been leading all day. He's fresh. If you see anything, don't get too close. I don't want anyone following us to know we're on to them."

Reb grinned as he hefted his saddle to the gelding's back. "You had me worried there a minute, J.D. I was afraid you didn't want me gettin' too close 'cause you was afraid I might get hurt."

"You can take care of yourself." J.D. glanced westward. It was the third member of their party that worried him.

Harlan sighted the five antelope a mile from camp. Reining downwind of the animals, he dismounted, tied the filly's reins to a rock, and moved toward the pronghorns on foot. As hard as he tried to put the day's events behind him, they replayed in his mind again and again. Life had a way of twisting things out of kilter and ripping them asunder.

Since Katherine had been taken from the Fort Stockton stage, he had acted out her rescue in his mind at least a hundred times. In each of those times, he was the man who freed her triumphantly from the kidnappers. And in each of those hundred rescues, Katherine McQuay, tears of joy and relief streaming down her lovely cheeks, hugged him closely and vowed eternal love.

He chided himself as he crept closer to the antelope. It was a childish, sentimental dream he nurtured, one that he should put behind him. Katherine and he were part of two different worlds now. He was nothing more than a West Texas ranch boy, and she was a lady. To be sure, when he was seventeen, he had attended a year of college back in the East Texas piney woods of Upshur County, but that did not bring him up to Katherine's level. She *was* a young lady, complete with a year of finishing school. Hers was a world of finery and high society, not horses and cattle.

Besides, the fantasy of singlehandedly pulling off Katherine's rescue had taken on for Harlan an especially perverse twist after today's debacle in the rock-strewn mountain pass. If twenty men, including his own father and two Texas Rangers, could not set Katherine free, who was he kidding in his dream about doing it all alone? The thought of her loveliness came back again and again.

Time to bury the past, he told himself. But he could not. He could not remember a time he had not loved Katherine—quietly loved her, never whispering his feelings or stealing an innocent kiss. Even as a boy he had sensed an invisible barrier between them whenever he had mustered the courage to tell Katherine of his love. She was a McQuay, daughter of Mr. J.D. McQuay—a man the whole county placed only a notch or two below God himself—and Caitlyn McQuay, a refined and cultured lady. He was merely a common Brewster.

College had been his mother's idea. Harlan had agreed to attend in the hope that he might better himself and somehow rise up to shine in Katherine's eyes. When his mother died at the start of his second year, he returned home for the funeral and remained in Monte Verde. By then he had learned enough to know that college would never give him the things he wanted, and it kept him far away from the land he loved. At nineteen he pinned a deputy's badge on his chest to help his sheriff father the way other young men would take up a desk job to help run a family business. And at twenty he purchased a half section of land and a handful of cattle, calling his place the Running B.

That same year, he watched Katherine leave Monte Verde for Austin. He was sure that he could put thoughts of Katherine behind him and find another girl to be his wife. He went to dances and picnics with several attractive and quite willing young girls, but Katherine always remained on his mind.

A twinge of guilt formed a knot in his belly. It had been so today when he rode into the pass beside his father. He had been daydreaming of Katherine when the first explosion ripped apart the wall of granite. Had he focused his thoughts on what was going on around him, he might have been able to save the men who died today—saved his own father. Now he was riding south to spill the blood of those who . . .

He caught himself. That was not it at all. He was riding to Presidio to find Katherine McQuay. She was the only reason he was here now.

A dog's bark brought him back from his reflections. General Lee bounded through the high grass to the south driving the pronghorns toward him. Harlan lifted Winchester to shoulder, took a bead on the lead antelope, and fired.

J.D. leaned over the campfire and sliced off a sliver of the roasting antelope backstrap with his hunting knife. He passed the sample to Harlan.

Popping the hot meat into his mouth, the younger man chewed for several seconds and then swallowed. "Tastes done enough to me."

Cutting a piece for himself, J.D. tried it. "We'll let it cook a little bit more and give Reb a chance to come in. If we don't, we'll never hear the end to his griping about us eating the choice cut while he was out working."

"You and Reb Boggs seem like a strange pair to be friends," Harlan said. "Since I can remember, he's barely managed to keep himself a step ahead of the law. Everybody in the county knows he's rustled more than a few head of cattle, as well as a horse now and then. Just nobody's ever been able to prove it."

J.D. chuckled as he settled cross-legged on the ground and poured himself a cup of coffee from a steaming pan sitting beside the fire. "Like as not no one ever will, either. Reb's not going to do anything that will get him caught—except maybe that old still of his, and I've never known anyone to complain about his shine."

"But rustling and horse thieving are against the law—they're hanging offenses," Harlan protested.

"Won't argue with you there, but did you ever notice how those who lose their stock to Reb don't complain all that much?" J.D. stared across the fire at the deputy.

"I've noticed, but I've never understood it," Harlan admitted.

"That's because every rancher around Marathon and Fort Davis owes Reb Boggs a thousand times over what he takes," J.D. said. "Whenever there was trouble, be it Comanches or Lipans or a storm that tore down a barn, Reb was always there for his neighbors. He never had a family of his own and sort of saw all of us as his family, I guess. Hell, if Reb ever got caught red-handed with a rustled steer, the ranchers hereabouts would swear on a stack of Bibles that they had never seen the brand on that steer, even if it was their own. I know I would, as would've your pa."

Harlan edged back his hat and stared at the campfire flames as though trying to absorb what J.D. had said. "If that's the way of it, why don't all of you just give Reb a little spread of his own and a small herd of longhorns?"

J.D. chuckled again. "Would make more sense, wouldn't it? But that isn't the kind of man Reb Boggs is. That would be charity and a mite too civilized, I reckon, for old Reb. You've got to understand that Reb has always seen himself as a loner capable of taking care of himself. At one time, he was. But those of us who came to this land, the ones he would have willingly given his life for, changed all that. We went and put brands on free-roaming cattle and mustangs. We made ranches out of what was once open territory. We, his friends, took away the very things Reb loved about this wild land."

"You make Reb sound like he was some kind of goldarn hero or something, 'stead of a common crook with a good heart," Harlan said with a shake of his head.

"He is a hero, but you won't find him written about in the history books. He never did anything grand enough for that. All he did was pull his friends' fat from the fire so many times that most of us lost count along the way," J.D.

replied. "Now we pay him back the way we can, in a way that's befitting the way he lives."

"Seems a bit convoluted, don't it?"

J.D. nodded. "Won't deny you that, but it works, and that's all that really matters."

Half asleep by the fire, General Lee abruptly came awake. His head snapped up, and his ears twitched to the north. A low growl rumbled in his throat.

"Call off your dog, J.D. It's only me," Reb called out.

Upon hearing the familiar voice, General Lee immediately settled back to the ground.

Riding beside the hobbled horses and mules, Reb dismounted, unsaddled the gelding, and then hobbled his own mount's front legs. He did not speak again until he squatted beside the fire and glanced at the roasting backstrap. "Well, I see I didn't get back none too soon. Given a minute more, you two would have had this et and left me to cook an old haunch on my own."

J.D. glanced at Harlan and winked. The young man smiled in reply.

"See anything?" J.D. asked as Reb sliced himself a portion of the meat.

"More than I wanted to see." Reb skewered the meat on the end of his hunting knife and chewed off a bite, not bothering with the tin plate J.D. placed on the ground beside him. "There's two campfires a-glowin' to the north, both about fifteen miles behind us."

"Two?" J.D. stared at the old scout. "Grand, just grand. We can't be sure of it, but I'd bet my last dollar that the men around those campfires are looking to relieve us of all this gold."

"Yep. One over to the northwest, the other to the northeast." Reb nodded as he worked the meat between his teeth. "This needs a pinch of pepper on it."

"Did you happen to get close enough to see how many men were around those campfires?" J.D. asked.

Reb wiped the grease from the corners of his mouth with the back of his hand and then shook his head. "You told me not to get too close—so I didn't."

J.D. pursed his lips and rubbed a hand over his chin.

"Could be that those to the northwest are following Caitlyn's decoy, but those to the east are after us sure as hell."

"You read it the way I do." Reb took another chew of the roasted antelope. "Looks to be that Caitlyn's decoy is workin' just fine, at least in part."

"Two fires," J.D. repeated as he looked at Harlan. The young man's expression said that he understood the implications of those fires. "Better eat all the antelope your belly can hold tonight. It'll be the last hot meal you'll get until we reach Presidio. We cold-camp from here on out."

The last of the flames in Tate Lansdale's low-burning fire winked out, leaving only the cherry-red glow of smoldering embers. Katherine studied the faces of her captors through an eye opened only to a slit. Lansdale and his men were asleep. All except Dwayne Holt, assigned to keep watch. And Holt was nodding. His eyelids grew heavy, slowly closed, and then blinked open to begin the process over again. Each time they closed, they stayed that way longer. It was just a matter of time before he drifted deeply into sleep.

He has to fall asleep! Has to! Katherine forced herself to maintain the ruse of sleep she had assumed shortly after Lansdale had ordered his men to bed down for the night. The posture was difficult to keep when every bone and muscle in her wanted to run screaming into the night. She had to control herself if she were to succeed.

This night would be her one and only chance to try her desperate plan. If she failed now, she was certain Lansdale would make sure she never had another opportunity.

Katherine slowly drew in a breath through her nostrils to quell the panic that rose within her once again. The mere thought of what she was considering had her temples pounding, and her heart lodged somewhere in the middle of her throat. Her mouth went cotton dry, and her palms were slick with sweat.

Young ladies do not sweat—they perspire, the voice of Virginia Brown, one of her teachers in Austin, echoed in her mind.

Mrs. Brown was wrong. Katherine sweated tonight. Her whole body prickled with sweat. She could smell herself, and what she smelled was the telltale sourness of fear. For that she felt shame.

So many times as a child she had heard adults tell of her mother and father standing off Comanche raiders. She expected such of men, but from a woman as dainty and beautiful as her mother feats of that magnitude seemed nothing short of heroic. What would Caitlyn McQuay think of a daughter who was petrified now with fear simply because she considered attempting to escape seven men who had kidnapped her? Katherine could well imagine the disdain in her mother's expression if she had known what was going on tonight in her daughter's mind.

But I am afraid—scared out of my mind, she admitted to herself.

The idea of attempting an escape had never entered her thoughts until this afternoon. All the time Lansdale and his men had held her captive on the mountain, even when they had ridden south, she had simply sat biding her time, knowing that any moment Els Brewster and the men of Monte Verde would ride in and free her.

This afternoon when Lansdale and the others had ridden on ahead to Goat Mountain, the reality of her situation had slapped her in the face. The men for whom she had patiently, confidently waited to rescue her were obviously dead—buried beneath tons of granite or shot down as they struggled to climb from the rocks Lansdale had sent crashing down on top of them.

It had taken every ounce of self-control she could muster to keep the tears that welled in her eyes from streaming down her cheeks as she listened to her captors brag and laugh about the men they had murdered en masse that afternoon. When she had recovered from the horror of those cold-blooded killings, Katherine was compelled to face her own situation—there would be no men coming to rescue her now. She was entirely on her own.

She did not doubt for a moment that her mother would somehow raise the huge ransom these men demanded. Nor did she doubt that the five hundred thousand dollars would be in Presidio according to their instructions. But

she did doubt that the men would release her after they
received the ransom. She knew their faces; she knew
every one of their names. She alone could identify them to
the law. Men such as Tate Lansdale, brutal as they were,
were far too smart to leave witnesses to testify against
them.

All of which added up to the fact that if she were to
live through this, her life now rested in her own hands.
Goat Mountain was a landmark she knew. She could get
back to the Circle Q from here. But if she delayed beyond
this night, Lansdale would be taking her into territory
with which she was totally unfamiliar. Each mile traveled
south would lessen her chances of ever seeing her home
again.

She opened one eye to a slit again and spied about
the camp. Although the red glow of the embers had
diminished, moonlight now bathed her captors' faces.
They still slept—the deep sleep of men who had not so
much as catnapped in forty-eight hours. She allowed a
smile to uplift the corners of her mouth when her attention shifted to Dwayne Holt. He no longer merely nodded
off; he was sawing wood. He leaned against a boulder, his
chin resting on his chest as he snored.

Still Katherine did not move. Instead, she slowly
counted to sixty fifteen times in succession, all the while
watching Holt to make certain the man still slept. Only
then did she roll to her side, gradually push to hands and
knees, and crawl fifteen feet away from the sleeping men
before summoning the courage to stand.

Her first inclination was simply to run into the night,
letting her legs carry her as fast and as far as they could.
She also knew no matter how fast or how far, it would be
neither fast nor far enough to outdistance seven men on
horseback. If she were going to escape, she had to have a
mount.

The horses stood twenty feet beyond the fire's glow-
ing embers—on the opposite side of the camp.

Moving one foot at a time, she swung in a wide circle
around the sleeping men. After pausing five times to make
certain her footsteps had not awakened her captors, she
reached the line of horses.

Again she bypassed her first inclination to mount the first bridled horse and ride northward bareback. Riding bareback did not bother her; it was leaving the other horses behind that did. As long as Lansdale and his band had mounts, they could and would follow her. To make certain her escape was clean, she had to let the remaining horses scatter, stranding her kidnappers on foot at least for a while—long enough to ensure her own safe escape.

She untied the reins of the first horse and quietly moved to the next. When she shifted to one side, allowing moonlight to bathe the knot in that second pair of reins, a hand shot over her left shoulder and clamped firmly down on her mouth, stifling the scream that tried to claw its way from her throat.

An arm snaked about her waist, squeezed and lifted her from the ground. She twisted and squirmed, to no avail. The arms holding her only tightened.

"Fightin' ain't gonna do you a bit of good this time, sweetheart—"

The blood in her veins turned to ice. The voice whispering in her ear belonged to Dwayne Holt.

"This time you're all mine!"

Her arms flailed behind her, slamming into his body. Her legs kicked, heels striking his shins. Neither slowed the determined Holt as he carried her into the night, away from his sleeping companions. He covered a full two hundred yards before his arms relaxed, and she spilled unceremoniously to the ground.

"Don't come near me!" she warned. "I'll scream. Lansdale will hear me and he'll put a bullet in your back."

A humorless smile slid across Holt's wet lips. "Go ahead and scream. It'll be the last sound you make." His right hand patted the pistol holstered on his hip. "I promise you that."

He was not bluffing; she saw that in his dark eyes. She swallowed back the scream that was ready to burst from her heart.

"I didn't think you wanted to die. 'Sides, what I got in mind most women like, once they get used to it." He chuckled, obviously enjoying her helplessness, the power he held over her. "A woman never looks right when she's wearin' men's clothes. Why don't you take that shirt and breeches off so I can get a real good look at you?"

Katherine did not move. Her mind raced. She had no desire to die, but she did not want to endure what Holt intended for her.

"I said get out of that shirt and breeches"—he patted the pistol to remind her of the alternative—"and do it now!"

A quiver of revulsion shot through Katherine's body as her fingertips rose to the first button of the shirt she wore and slowly worked it from its hole. Her eyes darted around, searching for—

A rock!

Three feet to her right lay a fist-sized stone. If she could reach the rock, she could open the side of Holt's head the moment he came to her. But how to reach the rock without being too obvious in her movements?

"I said now. Not tomorrow!"

Holt's right arm snaked out. His hand grasped the front of her shirt and wrenched.

Fabric ripped and buttons popped. He had torn right through the shirt and her lace-topped bustier.

"No!" Katherine's arms flew up, crossing themselves to cover her exposed breasts. She rolled to the right to hide herself from the leering eyes of this brute.

"Ain't no need to go and act shy on me now." Holt chuckled again. "You and me are gonna git to know each other real good 'fore this night's out."

Katherine's fingers crept out, found, and wrapped themselves around the rock. She drew it to her. Every muscle in her body tensed as she prepared for Holt to approach her.

"The only thing you're gonna get is a cracked skull if you go near her, Dwayne." Lansdale's voice came calmly from out of the night. "She just picked up a rock."

Katherine turned her head to see Holt spin around and face Lansdale, who stood twenty feet behind him. Holt's right hand hovered just an inch above the Colt on his hip.

"Tate, back off. This don't concern you none." A cold edge sharpened Holt's voice. "I caught her tryin' to make off with one of our horses, and I was gonna teach her a lesson."

"With your pants unbuttoned?" Lansdale asked, taunting him. "Reckon we both know exactly what you were intendin' to do with the girl, don't we, Dwayne?"

Holt did not answer, nor did his right hand move away from the gun.

"I told you what would happen if you went for the girl before we got the ransom," Lansdale said. "Did you forget, Dwayne?"

"I didn't forget," Holt answered. "I ain't gonna hurt her none, Tate. You just go on back to your sleepin' roll and let me handle this."

"I can't do that. You know that as well as I do, Dwayne. How could I expect the other boys to stay in line, if I don't stand by my word."

Katherine saw Lansdale's own right hand slowly inch toward the Colt on his right hip.

"Forget it, Tate. You're an old man. You ain't fast enough to take me," Holt challenged, but Katherine sensed a hint of uncertainty in his voice.

"Only one way to find out, Dwayne." She heard not even a trace of doubt in Lansdale's answer.

"Tate, I got no want to—"

Holt did not finish his sentence. His right hand dropped, closing around the revolver's grip.

Lansdale moved at the same time. Only he was quicker. His Colt cleared its holster and spat fire and lead before Holt could even free his weapon.

"Wha . . . " A surprised gasp quavered from Holt's lips. His gun slipped from his fingers and fell to the ground unfired.

A heartbeat later, Holt collapsed. His body jerked spasmodically in its pointless dance of death as he lay facedown in the sand.

Holstering the Colt, Lansdale walked past the fallen man and yanked Katherine to her feet.

"Sometimes, girl, when I consider how a female like you can rouse a man to fire, I get to thinkin' it might be easier to kill you and be done with it." He shoved her back toward the camp. "But as long as your momma's still got that half million waitin' for us . . ." His words trailed off. "I've got a needle and thread in my saddlebag. You can mend them buttons. And you had better mend 'em good. I don't want you temptin' none of my other boys and causin' a mutiny in the ranks. You hear me?"

Katherine stumbled forward, her arms clutching the open front of the shirt to her chest. She was barely cognizant of Lansdale's words. She had tried for freedom and failed. The courage she had gathered within her had all but evaporated; her spirit shriveled and cracked like a melon left too long in the sun.

Lansdale's hand clamped down on her shoulder like a steel vise. He jerked her around to face him and pulled her hands out to her sides. She was on display for him, completely vulnerable. "What you tried was stupid, girl. Do you understand that? I had to kill a man because of your stupidity."

His left hand dropped to his waist. Steel hissed against leather. There was a silvery flash in the moonlight as his hand jerked up—a glint of light that danced along the length of a hunting knife which he held a fraction of an inch from her nose.

"If you ever try to slip away on me again—if you ever even think about it—I'll use this on you, girl." His breath, hot and sour, burned in her face. "I'll cut the tendons in your ankles sure as I'm lookin' at you. Then you won't be able to run—or walk—again, ever, for the rest of your life. Your momma won't mind. She'll still pay to have you back. But you'll mind. You'll sure as hell mind! And so will any man fool enough someday to want you!"

Katherine's gaze focused on the razor-sharp steel. Lansdale now laid the cold blade right over her fast-pumping heart, against her naked breast. She understood his threat, but it did not matter. She had failed. And in her heart, she knew these men would never release her even when they received the ransom.

Lansdale spun her around and shoved her forward again. "Now get back to the camp. I've lost enough sleep over you for one night as it is."

Chapter Twelve

Grass-covered rolling hills strove to match the heights of the few true mountains sprinkled amid them. The hills soon gave way to arid flatlands that grew more rock and prickly pear cactus than they did grass. With each mile that J.D. and his two companions covered, the desolation only intensified.

The pronghorn antelope and mule deer that had been so plentiful a day's ride to the north were replaced hereabouts by mere jackrabbits and lizards. General Lee gave chase to each. Those he caught he ate as he plodded alongside the men, or else carried his quarry patiently in his mouth until the men paused to rest their mounts. Then he hastily devoured his prey.

J.D. made no attempt to hamper the mongrel's natural hunting instinct. General Lee displayed an admirable streak of common sense. Had J.D. been given the choice, he too would have preferred rabbits over the fare he now ate. Beef jerky and water three times a day quickly lost its charm as a menu. He would have passed up eating altogether had it not been for the rumbling protests of his stomach.

As tempting as roasted rabbit was, the temptation did not overrule caution. The two campfires Reb had sighted to the rear played on J.D.'s mind. Smoke during the day and the red-orange glow of flames at night would surely give away their position.

Not that those behind them would have any great difficulty following the trail laid down by ten mules and

110

four horses. He grimaced when he glanced back at the deep tracks the gold-burdened mules left behind them.

For an hour he had tried the old Comanche trick of tying brush behind the animals to obliterate their hoofprints. Although the brush worked, it raised such a cloud of dust that even a myopic greenhorn would have been able to spot them from far across the plain. J.D. had ordered the brush cut away.

That the men following them would strike was a certainty in J.D.'s mind; the only question was when. Had he been those behind, he would wait until the gold was closer to the Mexican border before striking. Such an attack would mean a shorter flight with the ransom loot across the Rio Grande and beyond the reach of Texas lawmen.

On the other hand, out here, away from any town, an attack would go unnoticed, and several routes to the border were open to men fleeing the law.

Not that J.D. planned to have the ransom taken from him, but he was trying to think like those trailing them. The problem was that this wild, open country offered too many opportunities for an ambush. The only way to proceed was on the assumption that an attack could come anywhere and at any time.

When they camped the second night, Reb once more rode to the north to scout the terrain behind them. He returned two hours later, reporting he sighted no campfires tonight.

J.D. knew better than to believe the men tracking them had given up. They had simply gone to cold-camping themselves to hide their position. That night J.D. kept guard while Harlan and Reb slept. He had not intended to stare wide-eyed at the surrounding countryside throughout the night, but his churning brain refused to allow sleep to come.

The third day saw the last of the grasslands. Creosote bushes anchored to the sand by a network of moisture-seeking roots dominated the harsh territory they moved through. They had entered the northern reaches of the Chihuahuan desert. And desert travel brought a whole new world of flora and fauna, strange even to a cattleman's experienced eyes. Where creosote did not grow, there were spindly ocotillo, thorned wait-a-minute, and yucca plants that bore the names Spanish dagger and bear grass.

Prickly pear was the most prolific of the cactus that sucked precious moisture from the soil, but its large flat pads took on strange forms hereabouts that were not to be found in other parts of Texas. Men had given the name blind cactus to pear that appeared to have no needles on its pads.

Long draws of sand and rock were common and could make the going tough, even for mules; but more common were broken hills and deeply eroded gullies. And there were mountains. Not gently sloping mounds covered in grass, like those found to the north. These were jagged fortresses of bare rock that thrust unannounced from the desert floor like the petrified, mangled bodies of monstrous leviathans.

Nor did piñon pines and junipers grow near the crests of these peaks, as was common in the Del Nortes and the Davis Mountains to the north. To find trees, real trees that could provide shade and a hiding place, a man had to climb high to reach the bowllike basins that sometimes separated the peaks of these mountains. Only there was enough moisture gathered from passing clouds to sustain lush vegetation.

Cinnabar, carrying precious mercury, and nickel were abundant in these mountains. Many men had come here hoping to make their fortunes mining the bountiful minerals, only to be broken in two like desiccated blades of grass caught in the desert wind. Few men walked out without paying a heavy price for the attempt. No railroad ran this far south, and maintaining the stock and wagons required to bring ore out of the desert had bankrupted a score or two of ill-informed investors.

"Even the Indians used to think of this place as hell." Reb shook his head as he scanned the rugged terrain. "The sooner we reach the Rio Grande the better it will be with me."

J.D. agreed, but the river still lay at least three days ahead of them. In between was nothing but desert. Had they not been leading the mules, they could have made the ride in half the time. As it was, they had covered but twenty-five miles each of their first two days on the trail.

Reb twisted around in the saddle and glanced over his shoulder. "Harlan's comin' in. He's 'bout a mile back."

J.D. nodded. He had sent the young man back to see if he could catch sight of the men on their tail.

"The boy seems to be workin' out all right," Reb said with a touch of surprise in his voice. "What worries me is how is he goin' to act when we meet up with those men that kilt his pa?"

"I've been giving that some thought, too," J.D. admitted as he peered overhead. "I haven't come up with any answers either. I reckon there's no way to judge what the boy will do until we reach Presidio."

The scattered white patches of clouds that had floated incongruously across a field of blue in the morning now gathered, forming ominous, dark, aerial mountains.

"Don't worry about them clouds none," Reb advised. "This is the Chihuahuan desert, remember. It ain't rained down here since Noah rode out the flood."

"You're probably right," J.D. agreed. "But a little rain would go a long way to cooling things off."

"And would wash away the trail we've been leavin'," Reb added.

Harlan rode up beside the two men and eased back on the reins to draw his mount to a walk. "There's rain back north, but that was all I could see."

"Grand." J.D. had hoped the young man would at least sight dust clouds on the horizon to give them some indication of how closely they were being followed.

"I'll hang back again, if you want," Harlan suggested.

J.D. shook his head. "Later maybe, but—"

Lightning flashed and thunder cracked, drowning his words. In the next instant raindrops the size of silver dollars fell from the clouds above them. None of the three men bothered with the slickers tucked in their sleeping rolls. The rain hit so fast and so hard that they were drenched in a matter of seconds. Tugging the wide brims of their hats low to their faces, they simply continued south, pushing horses and mules through the downpour as

fast as the rocky ground and nearly invisible horizon
would let them.

A half hour later, the rain stopped as abruptly as it
had begun. Within ten minutes puddles of standing water
had been sucked into the thirsty sand. Except for a cuppy
texture to the ground and the heavy, steamy air, the
passing storm had done nothing to change the face of the
desert, at least as far as J.D. could tell.

Then J.D. and his companions topped a rocky hill
and peered below. A wide arroyo, usually no more than a
dry gully, raged in front of them, in their path, with
muddy water that swirled and foamed as it sliced through
the compliant desert.

"A mite more rain fell than I thought." Reb turned
from the raging stream to J.D. "Never figured I'd see a
flash flood in this dried-out hellhole."

Neither did J.D., but a heavy rain in a desert had no
place to go. Although sand would greedily drink in any
moisture that fell upon it, rock would not. The Chihuahuan
desert was more rock than sand. The brief downpour had
produced enough runoff to flood the entire arroyo and
form a small river.

"It isn't more than thirty feet to the other side,"
Harlan said. "It can't be that deep. Let's see if we can't
cross it."

J.D. shook his head. "It isn't the depth we have to
worry about. It's the force of the moving water. That gully
has a rock bottom. If one of the mules or our horses were
to slip, we could lose them in a second. I can't risk that."

He glanced around and pointed to an overhang of
rock that shafted from the side of the hill. "The water'll go
down soon enough. We'll wait it out over yonder. It won't
hurt to give the stock a rest, and I could use a catnap
myself. That rock will keep the sun or rain off us, depend-
ing on what this weather decides to do next."

As they reached the overhang and dismounted, J.D.
studied the northern sky. Lightning leapt from dark clouds
to the ground and distant thunder rumbled in the air. He
saw sheets of rain washing across the land—water that
would work its way here to feed the raging stream below
them.

"Boys, we all might as well break out the sleeping blankets. Until that rain plays out we aren't going anywhere, and from the look of it, that'll be a while yet." He untied his bedroll and spread it on the ground, removing the shotgun it concealed and laying the weapon beside the blankets. "We'll make up the delay by riding hard tonight."

As he stretched out on top of the blanket, he looked up at his companions. "Decide among yourselves how you're going to handle the watch. Me, I'm going to sleep."

With that he tugged his hat brim over his eyes and was out....

Ten minutes later, it seemed, General Lee was growling in his ear, shattering a worried dream concerning two hundred head of saddle-broken mustangs that he was supposed to deliver to the U.S. Army in Santa Fe by the first of July.

J.D.'s eyes opened, not to sunlight, but to the shadows of a moonlit night. He blinked. He had slept for hours, not minutes.

His eyes darted about the campsite to find Reb standing near the edge of the overhang with shotgun in hand. General Lee stood poised at his side. The dog's ears were pinned back, his tail motionless. Harlan lay atop his own blankets a few feet away, still sleeping.

"What is it?" J.D. whispered.

"Don't know," Reb answered without looking back at his friend. "The General and me thought we heard somethin' move out there, but I'll be damned if either one of us can see a thing. Better nudge Harlan out of his dreams, just in case."

"Why didn't you wake me earlier?" J.D. asked as he reached over and gave Harlan's shoulder three quick shoves to awaken the young man while signaling him to keep quiet. "I didn't mean to sleep half the day away."

"No need to disturb you," Reb answered as J.D. crept beside him. "Stream's still up. Lightnin' didn't die away up north till a half hour ago or so."

Harlan joined the two older men. "What's up?" He only mouthed the words.

"Me and the dog thought we heard somethin' out there," Reb explained. "Only we don't see nothin'."

Neither did J.D. as his gaze traced the moonlight-washed hill where they were camped from its rocky crest to the still-raging river that rushed through the arroyo below. He glanced at the horses and mules tied twenty feet outside the overhang. "I'm going to get the rifles off our saddles, just in case. I'd feel a mite more secure with something that has a little more range than this shotgun."

He took two steps toward the horses when a blaze of blue and yellow spat at him from the rocks above. The crack of a rifle rent the night's silence. A cloud of sand and dust erupted at J.D.'s feet as a bullet buried itself in the ground.

He reacted rather than thought. Pivoting, he threw himself back beneath the overhang, disappearing in its shadows. With a grunt he flopped belly down beside his two companions.

Reb glanced down at him, his arched eyebrows visible in the moonlight. "Reckon the General and me was right after all about somethin' bein' out there."

"Some*one*," J.D. corrected without a hint of amusement in his tone when he shoved to his feet.

"Some*ones* would be my guess," Reb answered as his neck craned to get a better look at the hilltop. "Doubt if it's just one man up yonder."

Harlan, cocked pistol in hand, edged to the opposite side of the overhang and peered out. He shook his head to signal that he saw nothing.

"How many men are up there is the question." J.D.'s eyes scanned the rocky cover that hid their uninvited visitors. Nothing visible moved among the shadows.

"We could always ask 'em down for a cup of coffee to get a head count," Reb said. "Though I doubt that they're feelin' in a neighborly mood."

J.D. looked back at the stock. The twenty feet that separated him from the horses might as well have been a mile. In the time it would take him to cross to the rifles, those above could put a dozen slugs into him.

"You men down there," a voice called suddenly from above. "You men hear me?"

Harlan glanced at his companions. There was shock in

his voice when he whispered, "Damned if that don't sound like Johnny Griffin. I went to school with him."

"You're probably hearing right," Reb grunted. "But I wouldn't go and put too much weight in old friendships just now."

"You men down there, I said, can you hear me?" the voice called again.

J.D. nodded to Harlan. "Go ahead and answer him. Hearing your voice might be all it takes to make him rethink what he's doing."

"Wanna give me odds on that?" Reb asked.

"I hear you, Johnny Griffin," Harlan answered. "This here's Harlan Brewster. What are you after, Johnny?"

Nothing came from above for several seconds; when it did, the voice belonged to another man. "Deputy, we ain't lookin' to do no killin'. All we want is them mules and what's on 'em. Turn 'em over to us, and we'll let you three go free."

Reb looked at J.D. "That's Johnny's pa, Fred. I'm sure of it. An upstandin' member of the community and deacon of the Baptist church, if I recall rightly. You wouldn't strike a wager before, but how about a bet on how long we'd live if we did turn them mules over to him?"

"There wouldn't be time for either of us to pay off," J.D. said through clenched teeth. He then shouted in reply. "Fred Griffin, this is J.D. McQuay. I think you know that I can't let you have the mules. If you want them, the only way you're going to get them is to come down here and take them."

J.D. had chosen the space beneath the overhang with an eye to protect them from the elements. The site, halfway between the hilltop and the water below, now proved to be an excellent defensive position. There was only one way for the men above to get to them, and that was to come over the top.

Come they did. Whoops that imitated the war cries of raiding Comanches exploded from their chests as five men spurred horses from the rocks above and charged wantonly down the hillside. In the dim light J.D. could see the shower of sand and stone that flew from their mounts' hooves. Each man shouldered a rifle that he swung toward the rock overhang and fired at will.

Hot lead slammed into solid granite and ricocheted off the stone above J.D.'s head in a high-pitched whine and a hail of rock fragments. J.D., Reb, and Harlan threw themselves back and ducked, pressing flat against the rock to escape the volley.

The instant the last of the five shots rang out, they moved. Harlan and Reb leapt from beneath the overhang. One barrel of Reb's scattergun blasted. The second opened up while the deafening roar of the first was still ripping the air. At the same time, Harlan's Colt barked shots in rapid succession.

Simultaneously J.D. darted from the relative security of the overhang and ran for the horses. Both barrels of his own shotgun thundered as he whipped the muzzle of the weapon around in a wide arc and squeezed both triggers one after the other. He did not pause to see the effects of the barrage of buckshot and .45 caliber slugs. He *did* hear the screams of men and horses alike as he continued toward the rifles.

That short dash of a mere twenty feet turned into a nightmare. The hillside's uneven surface of rock and sand offered no solid footing for his racing boots. Each long stride of his legs became a wobbly misstep. His feet slipped and slid while his legs threatened to fly out from under him. Still he struggled forward, determined to retrieve the Winchesters from the saddle boots.

A single stretch of his legs separated him from his goal when a living mountain slammed into his side. As the force of the impact wrenched him from his feet, he glanced at that mountain from the corner of his eye. A riderless horse, forelegs thrown straight out and haunches buried in the sand, skidded toward the arroyo below.

J.D. spun full circle in the air before he hit the ground and tumbled downward. His arms flailed wide, and his fingers desperately sought a handhold to halt his own descent to the water below. At the same time, he dug the toes of his boots into the rock and sand. Nothing he tried impeded his downward rush. The half-buried boulder that suddenly crashed into his side did, though, driving the air from his lungs in a painful groan and jarring every bone in his body.

Shaking his head to fight off the exploding pinwheels of light that whirled in it, J.D. pushed up with his arms, pulled his legs under him, and stood. His eyes lifted.

Two horsemen, their rifles dipping toward him, barrels gleaming in the moonlight, charged down the hillside—or at least skidded straight at him. The horses were unable to overcome the momentum of the run down the sandy incline, and they slid rather than ran upright.

Charge or skid—it did not matter. Either way J.D. stood a fine chance of being crushed beneath the animals, if their riders' rifles did not cut him down first. Pulling the Colt from its holster, he took the only avenue open to him. He threw himself to the side and rolled.

Two rifles cracked, spitting fire and lead as he came to rest on his stomach. Bullets tore into the ground where he had stood but a heartbeat before. Lifting the Colt, he hastily pointed the revolver and fired at the closest gunman.

The rider screamed as lead slammed into his chest. Rifle flying from his hands, he fell from the saddle directly beneath the hooves of the horse of the second onrushing gunman.

J.D.'s only remaining shot caught the second of his attackers as the man cocked the lever of his rifle. Like the first, he died screaming when a .45 caliber slug tore straight into the center of his chest.

J.D. loaded with lightning-fast efficiency. Gun cocked and ready to meet a new attack, he once more scrambled to his feet.

But by now there was no attack, only Reb standing by the overhang shouting down at him, "You all right down there?"

"Yeah. I'm fine. How are you doing?" J.D. peered around, uncertain whether to believe his eyes.

The fighting was over. Two of the attackers' riderless horses climbed toward the hilltop with General Lee giving chase while three splashed across the stream below. The men who had ridden the animals lay sprawled on the ground, three near Reb and Harlan and two only a few feet from J.D.

"Yeah," he repeated. "I'm all right. Give me a report."

"Nary a scratch on either of us. Damned stupid thing for men to do, chargin' down a steep slope like that." Reb chuckled as he walked and slid down toward his friend. "Speakin' of stupid things, how come you run out like you did? Nearly got yourself kilt."

"I was . . ." J.D. waved his friend away. The rifles he had gone after were unimportant now, and J.D. was not one to acknowledge the old scout's sarcastic humor.

To the left Harlan rolled over onto their backs the two men whom J.D. had taken down in the hail of gunfire. He squatted beside each body and stared at the dead men's faces.

"Anythin' wrong?" Reb asked.

"I know all these men." Harlan stood, his head shaking in disgusted disbelief. "Every one of them is from town. They were all friends. I don't understand how they could have done something like this. They were good, law-abiding men. Not one of them ever caused a bit of trouble, not even a barroom fight on a drunken Saturday night."

"It's easy gold they was drunk on, son," Reb said. "Or what a man sees as easy gold. It brings the worst out in most men. A man will kill his own brother if he thinks he can get rich from it."

Harlan suddenly spun around and ran a dozen steps before he clutched his stomach with both arms and doubled over, retching.

Reb started toward the younger man, but J.D. reached out and grasped his shoulder to stop him. "Let him be. It isn't an easy thing for a man to find out that people he's known all his life aren't what they seem."

Reb looked back at his friend and nodded. "Reckon you're right."

General Lee barked above. J.D. glanced up. The mongrel stood beside the two horses that had disappeared over the hill a few moments earlier. Across the narrowing stream below, the three other horses had muzzles to the ground, foraging for nonexistent grass.

"There's still another group of men somewhere behind us," J.D. said. "They were bound to have heard all the shooting and might decide this would be a mighty good time to make a move."

"I've got your drift. I'll ride back and take a look just to be on the safe side," Reb answered.

While his friend mounted and rode northward, J.D. walked over to Harlan, who now sat on the ground staring at the stream below. "You all right?"

"More ashamed than anything," the young man said without looking up.

"Ashamed?" J.D. squatted at Harlan's side.

"About gettin' sick to my stomach the way I just did," Harlan answered. "I've never killed a man before—never even shot at one. I didn't know it was so hard. I knew those men, Mr. McQuay. They were friends."

J.D. eased his hat back on his head and rubbed a hand over his perspiring, mud-streaked face. He remembered the first man he had killed, an Apache warrior, and his own upheaving stomach that followed. It never was any harder than that, nor did it get any easier. "Harlan, there aren't any words to make what we had to do palatable. It goes down bitter no matter how you chew it. All I can tell you is, friends don't come gunning for a man. You, Reb, and I did what we had to do to stay alive. We didn't go after them; they came at us."

Harlan did not answer.

"And as to feeling ashamed, there's no reason for it," J.D. added. "The time a man should worry is when his stomach doesn't get all tied up in knots over killing another man." He glanced at Harlan. "Now, if you feel up to it, I need a hand rounding up those five horses."

Harlan touched the brim of his hat in what could have been a salute but was just a way of signaling thanks and that yes, he understood.

The arroyo was no more than a wide swath of mud when Reb reappeared on the top of the hill. Letting his horse slowly pick its way down to the overhang, he dismounted.

"They're still behind us," he announced. "Hangin' 'bout ten miles to our rear. They don't seem to be too.

worried about us knowin' it, either. They got a campfire blazin'."

"Could you make out how many there are?" J.D. asked.

Reb shook his head. "Didn't get that close. Didn't see any reason to push things. We've had enough bad luck for one night."

J.D. could not argue with that. Still, the situation would have rested easier on his shoulders if he knew exactly what they'd be up against if another attack came.

"You two have been busy." Reb's head tilted to five rock mounds visible in the moonlight.

"It was for their families, not them," Harlan said, his eyes recounting the graves. "It will help the good women-folk back home to know their men received a proper burial."

J.D. saw a shadow of disgust darken Reb's face. The older man would have done as J.D. had wished: He would have left the bodies where they had fallen. But Harlan was of another, gentler generation. And that, as J.D. saw it, was probably a step in the right direction for all of Texas, maybe all of the West.

"Look, gentlemen, we've got no more time for senti-mentality," J.D. said. "We've spent longer here than I wanted. Let's put some more miles between us and those behind before the sun comes up."

With that the three mounted and moved toward the southwest. While the older men led the gold-loaded mules, Harlan now handled a string of five new riderless horses.

Chapter Thirteen

The gently sloping incline ran for miles ahead of the six mounted men who led a young, auburn-haired woman astride a bay filly along the sandy bluff. Although the men's arms and hands moved freely to gesture as they spoke, the woman's did not. Hers were bound tightly with rope to the saddle horn. Nor did the woman speak; she had nothing to say to these men, her kidnappers.

That was just as well with Tate Lansdale, who eyed Katherine McQuay with a sidelong glance. Since the second night of the ride from the Del Norte Mountains to Presidio, the girl had not said more than a dozen words—usually just a hissing yes or no when she was asked a question.

At first Lansdale had thought Katherine's silence to be a submissive ruse to lull him into dropping his guard while she waited for another opening to escape. He, of course, had tripled his precautions with the girl. She was too valuable, too smart, too damn good-looking not to. She now rode with arms bound and slept with both arms and ankles secured with rope.

Now, graced with hindsight, Lansdale realized the girl's silence was not an act. Something had happened the night Holt had taken him on, in that struggle over a few moments' pleasure with her. What that something was, he was not certain of, but Katherine McQuay had changed. She had grown quiet and scared.

Scared, the thought repeated in his head. Maybe that was it; she was scared. *With damned good reason*. The smile that touched the corners of his mouth contained all

the warmth of the first blue norther of an oncoming
winter.

"That's it down yonder, ain't it?" Kelly Carter jabbed
a finger toward the south. "That's Presidio, ain't it?"

Lansdale's gaze briefly studied the faces of the five
men riding with him. An unforeseen benefit that stemmed
from his having shot Dwayne Holt was an abrupt shift in
the respect he commanded from these men. When he
gave an order, they snapped to and carried it out. Nor did
they even glance at the girl with more interest than a man
would look at a sack of flour or a bushel of potatoes.

He liked that, liked the feel of respect, even from
lowlifes such as these. When he had his hands securely on
Caitlyn McQuay's money, he would command a lot more
respect, and in wider circles, too. Once he was in Brazil,
everyone would be bowing and scraping. Tate never thought
to ask himself how he could safely transport that much
illegitimate cash all the way to South America. All he
knew was that with half a million American dollars—worth
over a million south of the border—people would ask,
"How high?" whenever he said, "Jump."

He liked that thought even more.

"Don't ask me," Todd Carter, Kelly's brother, said. "I
never been this far south 'fore."

Lansdale's eyes shifted, his gaze tracing down the
incline. At the bottom of the wide valley lay a narrow band
of water—the Rio Grande. On each side of the river was a
wide swath of green formed by the trees and grass that
drew life-giving moisture from the river. It was amid that
green that the white-washed adobe buildings of their
destination were clustered.

"Yep," Lansdale said, his smile growing at the thought
of the fortune that would soon be his. "That's Presidio. It
don't look like it's changed much since I was there back in
'80."

He did not mention that his first visit to Presidio had
been a quick one. He had merely passed through. His
goal had been the river, or the other side, as the case
happened to be. He had been escaping a five-man posse
that had chased him all the way down from Candelaria.
For a measly two hundred dollars, he thought, recalling

the paltry sum that the Candelaria bank had in reserve the day he chose to rob it. Now, when he crossed the Rio Grande again, Tate mused confidently, he would be carrying a vastly larger sum. Nor would he ever ride back into Texas and expose himself to danger. He would just head south until he reached safety and the good life in South America.

"Where's that old army fort you was tellin' us about, Tate?" Ray Powell turned to Lansdale. "I don't see nothin' but a handful of flat-roofed Mexican shacks."

Lansdale tilted his head to the left. "It's downriver, ten or so miles to the east. Ain't nobody in town goin' to be watchin' when we get the money. I planned it that way so we could keep everything all nice and quiet-like."

"Do we ride into town or head for the old fort?" Hank Yoakum asked.

"You and Ray ride into Presidio. The rest of us will swing wide around the town and aim for the fort," Lansdale replied, handing the man a twenty-dollar gold piece. "I want you to pick up some fresh supplies, enough to hold us over for a few days. It wouldn't hurt none to get somethin' a man can drink other than water. I ain't got no taste for pulque, but tequila's almost all right."

When Yoakum grinned from ear to ear with obvious delight, Lansdale added, "Don't go gettin' enough to make us blind, just a bottle or two to cut the dust from our throats. Understand?"

Yoakum's face sobered immediately and he nodded. "Understood, Tate."

Lansdale glanced at Powell and received the same nod of assurance. "Supplies ain't the only reason you're goin' into town. I want one of you to get a room somewhere. Seems I remember a cantina that's got rooms—or maybe a boardin' house. Don't matter what, just get a room. Choose between you as to who's goin' to stay, but I want one of you in town, keepin' his eyes open. Soon as our fortune comes ridin' in, I want to know about it."

Ray Powell glanced at Hank Yoakum. "Flip that gold eagle. Heads and I'll stay in that room."

As Yoakum did and came up tails, Billy Crow said, "There is no reason for either Ray or Hank to stay in

Presidio. I can hide down there among those rocks. Anyone coming in from the north will have to pass by. They will not be missed."

Lansdale looked at the maze of boulders halfway down the slope. Billy's suggestion had merit. A man and a horse could easily keep under cover among them.

But Lansdale dismissed the idea with a shake of his head. He did not trust the old Indian. Billy was liable to get a notion that he was a young Apache again and try to take the ransom for himself. Neither Ray nor Hank had enough brains or courage to try to cross him.

Looking back at the two he had chosen to ride into the border town, Lansdale tilted his head to the south. "You two go on. Ray, I'll expect to see you at the fort with those supplies by sundown. If you aren't there, I'll come lookin' for you."

"I'll be there," Ray answered as he nudged his mount forward.

As the two men rode toward Presidio, Lansdale reined his horse eastward, signaling the others to follow. The whole plan was working out perfectly.

The sun hung a hand's breadth above the western horizon when Lansdale and his men brought their precious captive at last to the fort's crumbling walls. In its state of decay and ruin it was difficult to imagine the fort in its former glory with adobe walls encompassing a full acre of land. It was even harder for Lansdale to conceive of why such a fort had been constructed in the first place.

Ten buildings—or what had once been buildings—still stood within the walls. None had roofs any longer and half had collapsed, leaving only a portion of their walls standing. Still, Lansdale rode to each one, examining it carefully. A decaying wall might not offer much shelter from the elements, but it would provide sufficient cover in a fight. It could also hide a man stupid enough to attempt to sneak up on them.

From the five structures still intact, Lansdale selected a long, low-slung building near the western wall as a campsite. The structure appeared to have once been a

stable and offered easy concealment for men and horses
alike.

He had Katherine placed in a smaller building closer
to the Rio Grande. Little more than a windowless shed, it
might once have been used to store supplies or ammunition. He left Billy Crow guarding the girl, with orders that
she be kept under constant watch, with the men sharing
the duty on two-hour shifts. Scared she might be, but he
was taking no chances with her trying anything with the
ransom coming so close now. Lansdale knew that frightened people had the bad habit of attempting stupid things.

By the time the sun began to sink and Ray rode in
from town, the Carter brothers had a campfire ablaze and
ready for the fresh beef and beans brought from Presidio.
But it was the distinctive, resonating sound of a cork being
pulled from a virgin tequila bottle rather than the tempting aroma of roasting meat that magnetized the men
around the fire.

"It'll be two weeks come tomorrow." Ray downed a
swallow of the golden-hued liquor Lansdale passed him,
then passed the bottle on to Todd Carter. "You think the
money will be in town by now?"

Before Lansdale could answer, Kelly Carter said, "It
damned well better be there. If it ain't, we kill the girl just
like we warned 'em we would."

Ray sat back on his bootheels. "That don't make much
sense. What if somethin' happened between Monte Verde
and here? Say a horse broke down or somethin'. That's
enough to slow men down and make 'em late. Shootin' the
girl would kill our chances of gittin' that money."

Kelly's brow furrowed as though he had not thought
of the possibility Ray posed. He scratched at his chin.
"But what's the purpose of threatenin' to kill that girl if we
don't intend to do it?"

The men turned to Lansdale to untie this knot, as he
sucked down another fiery swallow of tequila. He pursed
his lips and smacked them with decided relish.

"You're worryin' your mind over somethin' that ain't
never gonna happen," he finally said. "The money will be
there. I'll bet my full share against any of yours on that."

He paused for a moment and surveyed the faces of his

men. Each of his companions glanced away. There were no takers for his wager. They knew better than to gamble with anything Tate Lansdale said.

He smiled and took another swig from the bottle before handing it over. "But that girl ain't got long to live no matter when the money shows up in Presidio."

The comment snapped the three men's heads back to him. It was Ray who asked the question he knew would come. "What d'ya mean?"

He resisted the urge to shake his head. He had not selected these men because of their brains, but for the fact they would follow him. "You boys like Texas?"

The three nodded, looking sideways at one another uncomprehendingly. Then Kelly Carter asked, "What's that got to do with the girl?"

Lansdale bit his lower lip. None of the men had really considered the consequences of their actions. They lived their lives from one minute to the next, never thinking about what the following day would bring. Lansdale did; that was why he had managed to stay alive all these years in a rough line of work when other men—bolder men, men faster with a gun—were long dead and buried.

"Kelly, that girl's been with us two weeks now. Do you think she would recognize you if she ever saw you again?" Tate asked.

The man's brow creased deeply again.

Ray sucked at his lips, and Todd whistled softly as what Lansdale said sank in.

"She knows all our names and faces," Lansdale continued. "Unless you want to spend the rest of your lives lookin' over your shoulders, scared that you'll find the law ridin' down on you, we have to kill the girl."

"That's the way of it," Ray agreed. "Either that or take to Mexico until we die."

Todd shook his head. "I've been down in Piedras Negras. I ain't got no want to live in no Mexico."

"Me neither," Kelly said. "I was set on usin' my share of the money to buy me a spread up near Fort Worth or maybe out by Abilene."

"That's why we have to kill the girl," Lansdale said,

and then added, "and the men who bring us the money. They'll get a gander at our faces, too."

He did not give his men the opportunity to question him or to ponder the gravity of the action he had decided they would take. Instead he pointed to the various positions around the fort, telling each man where he would be hidden when the gold was brought in.

"We'll handle it quick and clean—no long drawn-out fight. They won't stand a chance. Then we'll kill the girl," Lansdale concluded. "We can divvy up the money that's rightly ours and be on our own way within an hour after that."

Again he watched the men nod their approval of his plan. When he accepted the half-empty tequila bottle, he took two big swallows. Everything he had told the three was the way it would happen, all except the last part—dividing the money and riding their separate ways. Tate Lansdale had never had any intention of splitting the ransom with anybody or letting anyone but himself ride away from the fort alive—and rich.

Chapter Fourteen

P_residio_. The name meant "fort" in Spanish. The Mexicans who had first settled along the Rio Grande called the town Presidio Del Norte, the fort of the north. Why they had, J.D. did not know or recall ever knowing. He had been to the border town but twice in his life, both times chasing Mexican rustlers.

Before the War Between the States, the U.S. Army had built a fort downriver from the town, calling it Fort Leaton, but Presidio had already been established as the town's name long before that. Perhaps the Mexicans, or the Spanish before them, had garrisoned troops here on the river as a defense against Apache and Comanche raids into the state of Chihuahua.

Nor was this town the first Presidio in the Big Bend region. Once before, the Spanish had established a settlement they called Presidio in Texas. It lay farther north, near the present site of Marfa. Older than even Florida's St. Augustine, that Presidio represented the earliest European settlement within the borders of what became the United States. It was a fact J.D. was certain most residents of Florida would dispute and the majority of Texans did not even know.

It was not that all-but-forgotten Presidio of times past that stood at the center of J.D.'s thoughts as he and his companions approached the whitewashed buildings that were present-day Presidio. In response to the kidnappers' demands, he was bringing half a million dollars to this border town exactly two weeks after Katherine had been taken from the Fort Stockton stage.

Saddle leather creaked to J.D.'s left as Reb twisted around in the saddle and stared behind them. When he turned back, he looked at his friend. "Still no sight of them that's been tailin' us. Do you reckon they saw the five graves we left back by that arroyo and changed their minds about tryin' to take this gold away from us?"

"I've been thinking the same thing," J.D. answered. "If they haven't, they've waited too long to make a move. By God, we're here."

They passed an adobe shack with a front yard filled with three barking dogs, five kids, and a dozen chickens, all of which General Lee arrogantly ignored. The owner of the house, a mustached young man in white cotton shirt and breeches and leather sandals, stood in the doorway watching them. His attention centered on the mules they led.

"That's a long and hungry look if I ever saw one," Reb said with a shake of his head.

The expression became one with which they quickly became familiar. It was on the face of every man and woman they passed as they rode toward the center of Presidio. People gazed hungrily at the mules and merely glanced at the three men who rode with loaded rifles ready in hand.

"I don't like the look of this," Harlan said softly. "Everybody in town knows what we're carrying on the mules."

"And probably most of the children," J.D. said with a grunt of disapproval.

They had Els to thank for that, J.D. realized, as he remembered Els's mentioning that he had notified the local authorities of Katherine's kidnapping. He had probably detailed the size of the ransom in the same telegram. Even if he had not, two weeks was a long time to keep such news under wraps. News like this spread around the territory via the proverbial grapevine faster than it moved by wire.

Reaching the junction of Presidio's two main streets, J.D. halted and quickly scanned the wooden shingles hanging from the storefronts. The town still had not grown large enough for a hotel, but a cantina to the right proclaimed, on its gaudily painted sign in red, yellow, blue, and green, that it had rooms for fifty cents a night. J.D. tilted his head toward the cantina. "We have to get off the street with this gold, and that looks as good a place as any."

He left Reb and Harlan outside as he entered the cantina, one of three two-story buildings in town. The proprietor, a middle-aged Mexican with a drooping mustache and cheeks and chin that had not been shaved in two days, stood behind the bar of a one-room saloon. Two customers sat at one of the tables within. They barely glanced up from their conversation when J.D. walked straight to the bar.

"How many rooms do you have upstairs?" J.D. nodded to the wooden stairs at the back of the cantina that led to the second floor.

"Four, señor." The man took a bottle of tequila and a glass from behind the bar and placed them on the varnished wood before J.D.

Waving the drink away, J.D. said, "I want to rent all four of them for the next couple of nights." It was the only way he knew of assuring relative privacy and security for the gold outside.

The cantina keeper's eyes widened. "All four, señor? I have never had a man make such a request. Usually the men who come here merely wish to visit one of the rooms for an hour or so with Rosita or Maria, who work for me. You look to be a man of the world and surely understand." He winked slyly.

"I still want all four rooms." J.D. understood, but with a life's earnings in gold to protect, he could not be concerned with the usual activities that went on in the cantina's rooms.

"I cannot accommodate you, señor." The cantina's proprietor shook his head. "Rosita and Maria are poor working girls. I could not turn them out."

The man was no doubt more concerned with his cut of the money the two women earned than turning them out of the rooms, J.D. surmised. To satisfy the man's greed, J.D. dug into a pocket and brought out three gold pieces. He placed the first on the bar. "This is for the rooms. I shouldn't be needing them for more than a night—two at the most."

The barkeeper stared at the twenty dollars and then looked at the two coins still in J.D.'s hand. "And those, señor?"

J.D. stacked the two coins, five-dollar pieces, atop the first. "These are for Rosita and Maria as compensation for their inconvenience."

The proprietor's hand moved to scoop up the thirty dollars. He froze with his fingertips a fraction of an inch from the money. His shoulders sagged, and he sighed heavily. Disappointment shadowed his face. "I am truly sorry, señor. As much as I would like to accommodate you, I cannot. One of the rooms is rented to a Señor Yoakum. While Maria and Rosita can stay with relatives, Señor Yoakum is a visitor to our town and has nowhere else to go."

Reaching into his pocket a second time, J.D. brought out another gold piece, another twenty dollars this time, that he placed on top of the others. "Surely, there is a home in town that takes boarders. I'm certain that you can find Mr. Yoakum a place to spend the night."

A wide grin spread beneath the man's dark mustache, and his face brightened. "How stupid of me! I forgot that my sister Juanita has a spare bedroom that she often rents to travelers." He snatched up the coins and deposited them in his own pocket. "Give me an hour and all four rooms will be yours."

"Make it half an hour," J.D. said. "Meanwhile, my men and I will begin moving into the vacant room."

"Men, señor?" The man arched an inquisitive eyebrow.

"Two men besides myself," J.D. said, and then added, "and one dog."

Refusing to give the cantina owner time to find another angle to increase the price of the rooms, J.D. turned and walked outside. He pulled his shotgun from the bedroll behind his saddle and handed it to Reb. "You've pulled guard duty while Harlan and I get these boxes inside."

Reb stepped from the saddle and slipped the scattergun from his own bedroll. A cocked double-barreled shotgun in each of his hands, the old scout took a position in front of the cantina.

At J.D.'s signal General Lee sat on his haunches beside the mules, watching the street for any of the townsfolk whose curiosity about the contents of the boxes might overrule their sense of caution.

Alternately hauling one of the gold-coin-laden boxes up the stairs and standing watch over the boxes that had been placed in the vacant room, J.D. and Harlan managed to complete their task by the time the proprietor persuaded Rosita and Maria, with the help of ten dollars each, to vacate their rooms. Señor Yoakum did not relinquish the fourth room so easily. He finally departed after spewing a string of vehement curses at J.D. and the barkeeper, in spite of the latter's assurance that the room waiting for him in Juanita's home was far more comfortable.

As Yoakum stormed from the cantina, Reb glanced into the room he had abandoned. Its furnishings were spartan—a simple bed and a single chair. "Never seen a man so attached to a bed and a chair before, J.D."

"I noticed that myself," J.D. answered, but did not have time to give the man's reaction a second thought.

Harlan asked, "Does each one of us take the remaining three rooms?"

"All three of us stay in the room with the gold," J.D. said with a shake of his head. "Let's just hope the floor holds up under all this weight. I rented the other rooms to keep things simple. The fewer people we have around the boxes, the easier it will be." J.D. pointed to the bedroom's single door and single window. "There's two of you and two entrances to this room. Both of you should be able to make sure no one comes through either while I'm gone."

"Gone?" Reb's face twisted in question.

"I'm going to see about getting our stock grained and bedded down," J.D. answered. "After that, I thought the General and I might take a stroll around town just in case there's someone here that has a message for me."

Reb frowned. "I don't like us splittin' up that way, J.D. You're puttin' yourself in the open for anyone who gets the notion to take a potshot and eliminate a third of the opposition standin' between him and this here gold."

"I don't relish it much myself. But I don't see any other way to it." J.D. shrugged. "I'll bring hot food when I come back."

On the street J.D. left horses and mules hitched outside the cantina and called General Lee to heel as he walked down Presidio's streets. He found a livery stable at the western end of town and paid the owner twenty dollars to gather the animals in front of the cantina and care for them. He then handed the man another twenty and added, "Keep their tack close at hand and your barn doors open. I'm not certain when I'll have to ride again, and I want to be ready to move out day or night."

"For twenty dollars, señor, you can have your horses and mules whenever you want them," the stable's owner said with a wide grin. "The horses will be in my barn and the mules in the corral behind the barn." The man pointed westward to an adobe house a quarter of a mile to the west of the livery stable. "That is my home. If you need me at night, I will be there."

Bidding the man good day, J.D. walked back down the street with General Lee at his side.

Presidio had changed little since he had last been here nearly eight years ago. Built at the confluence of Cibolo Creek and the Rio Grande—a joining of two streams when it rained enough to send water running down the usually dry gully that was the Cibolo—Presidio's homes and a double handful of shops and stores were built along only two streets.

The main avenue ran north and south. Northward it led to the desert, the prairie, and eventually Monte Verde. South, across the Rio Grande, was the Mexican town of Ojinaga, a community almost three times as large as Presidio with its five hundred residents.

The east-west street led to a road that meandered with the banks of the Rio Grande. Riding west would take a man through the Chinati Mountains to the small towns of Indio, Ruidosa, and Candelaria. Beyond that was nothing but mile upon mile of open territory until distant El Paso. To the east lay the towns of Redford and Lajitas.

J.D. reached the junctions of these two streets, stopped, and took in the whole town one dusty avenue at a time.

The attention he and his companions had drawn when
they rode into Presidio now focused on him. He could feel
the eyes of merchants and storekeepers peering at him
through the curtained windows of their shops. Passersby,
men and women alike, scrutinized him with intense interest as they strolled down the streets. He even drew
another angry glare from Señor Yoakum, who rode eastward from town on the back of a chestnut.

Moving up and down each of the streets, J.D. made
certain that he was quite visible, should any of the kidnappers decide to contact him. At the same time, he carefully
noted alleys, open areas, and abandoned buildings, mem-
orizing their locations. He was preparing himself with a
mental map, so that when the time came for the exchange
of money for Katherine, he would be prepared to retreat
quickly and make a stand—should the need arise.

As much as J.D. prayed that such a need would not
materialize, he was ready for the worst. Men brazen
enough to kidnap a young woman, kill one man and
wound another, set off a murderous landslide, and demand
five hundred thousand in ransom were capable of anything. It was that anything he dreaded.

Neither a stop in a barbershop for a trim and a shave
nor visits to Presidio's two general stores brought the
contact with the kidnappers he hoped for. Before walking
back to the cantina, he entered a small café, ate a fried
steak and bowl of pinto beans, and then ordered a tray
with similar meals for Harlan and Reb. Both men
relinquished their guard duty to J.D. and General Lee
when man and dog returned to the room.

"You ain't got the look of a happy man, J.D.," Reb
said as he sat on the edge of the bed and hungrily attacked
the steak that filled the plate balancing precariously on his
knees.

"I've been through this town twice—and nothing," he
answered. "The men that brought us here are either blind
or yellow—or just cautious as hell."

"Maybe they don't even know we're here," Harlan
suggested.

"They'll get in touch with us when they're ready,"
Reb said around a mouthful of meat, casting the young

man a dubious glance. "I doubt that they could've missed us when we rode into town. Nobody else did."

J.D. stared out the window to the street below. The eyes of every man and woman who passed turned up and stared at the second story of the cantina. It had not taken long for word to spread through the small town that three strange men with a score of heavy, padlocked boxes were staying in the cantina. Like Reb, J.D. was certain the kidnappers knew both they and the gold were in Presidio. "It's their move now. All we can do is wait."

The possibility of a long wait sat heavily on his mind. The longer they stayed in Presidio, the greater the chance that some of the locals would decide that three men were a small obstacle to overcome when there was half a million dollars to be gained. From the covetous, hangdog looks he saw on the faces of the town's residents, he doubted that many in Presidio would come to their aid. If anything, the opposite would be true. The whole town just might join in on a raid and try to separate them from the gold.

Below, a man crossed the street and walked directly toward the cantina. Sunlight glinted off a badge pinned to the front of his shirt.

J.D. turned from the window and looked at Harlan. "Did Els have a deputy stationed here in Presidio?"

The young man shook his head. "They've got a town sheriff named Carlos Tinajas. Why?"

"Do you know him by sight?" J.D. asked.

Harlan nodded and again asked, "Why?"

"We're about to have a visitor," J.D. answered. "I want to make certain the man who's going to knock on that door is a lawman."

Harlan's mouth opened, but his words went unspoken. All three men turned as they heard from outside the heavy sound of boots climbing the wooden stairs. Those footsteps grew nearer, ending with a knock at the door.

Harlan and Reb set aside their unfinished meals and lifted their shotguns, while J.D. moved beside the door. "Who is it?"

"Sheriff Carlos Tinajas," the man outside answered. "If you men are from Monte Verde, I've come to offer my assistance."

J.D. glanced at Reb and Harlan, who cocked the hammers of their scatterguns. He then unlocked the door and opened it.

The sheriff's smile evaporated from his face, and he froze with one foot halfway across the threshold when his eyes alighted on the two shotguns leveled at his belly. His hands jerked high in the air above his head.

J.D.'s glance shot to Harlan, who looked at the sheriff and said, "Carlos, it's been a few years since you've ridden up Monte Verde way."

"Longer since you or your father visited Presidio, Harlan," Tinajas answered, lowering his arms when J.D. signaled his companions to set aside their weapons and waved the lawman into the room.

As Harlan began the introductions, J.D. closed the door and relocked it. "How can we help you, Sheriff?" he asked when he shook the man's hand.

"It is I who wish to help you, Mr. McQuay." Though his accent was decidedly Mexican, Tinajas's grammar was formal, apparently befitting what he saw as his elevated rank in town. "Harlan's father wired me of your daughter's kidnapping and the ransom demanded by those who abducted her." The sheriff nodded at the boxes. "I assume that those contain the ransom and you are here to deliver them. I extend the service of myself and my office to assist you in any way that I can."

J.D. pursed his lips thoughtfully and shook his head. "It's a neighborly offer, Sheriff Tinajas, but I'd rather you stayed out of this. The three of us can handle what needs to be done."

Surprise mixed with shock washed over the lawman's face. "Surely you are joking, Mr. McQuay?"

"It's no joke, Sheriff." J.D.'s stare met Tinajas's eyes squarely. "The last time men wearing badges tried to involve themselves in this, it cost more than a dozen of them their lives, including your lawman friend Els Brewster. I'd just as well not have any more men dying, thank you very much."

Tinajas frowned and looked at Harlan, who nodded in agreement, explaining what had occurred in the mountain pass. "Now we're handling this Mr. McQuay's way."

The sheriff's shoulders sagged. "But without doubt there is something—"

J.D. did not allow him to finish. "You can tell me if there've been any strangers in town lately."

"Presidio is a border town, Mr. McQuay; you know that," Tinajas said. "There are always strangers here. They come and go each day. Half of them are running away from something in Texas or Mexico. So one man, even two could enter this town and not be noticed. But seven men with one young woman would be unusual. That I would notice, and that I have not seen."

Walking back to the window, J.D. glanced outside once more. The long shadows of evening crept across the street. It would be dark within half an hour, and as yet he had no indication whatever that Katherine and her kidnappers had come to Presidio. There was nothing he could think of to do, except to sit and wait.

Three more times Tinajas tried to convince J.D. that he could raise whatever number of men were needed to successfully free Katherine from her captors. And three times J.D. refused the offer. Finally the sheriff gave up, and with a rhetorical flourish invoking the aid of both St. Christopher and St. Jude, he bade the three good luck and good night.

"What now?" Harlan asked when J.D. locked the door behind the flowery Tinajas.

"We do just what we're doing now—we wait," J.D. said dryly. "If that isn't enough, we'll wait some more."

Except for the candles that burned in the windows of a few homes sprinkled through the town, Presidio slept, which was why J.D.'s attention centered on the lone horseman who rode toward the cantina. The man stared up at the second story as he approached, stopping his mount precisely when he reached the front door of the cantina.

"Reb, Harlan, we've got ourselves a nighttime visitor. Looks like something's up." J.D.'s pulse raced. "There's a rider outside."

In the next instant J.D.'s stomach sank. The man

below looked away, nudged his horse's sides, and moved on.

"False alarm," J.D. made no attempt to disguise the disappointment in his voice. "He rode by. I can't see another soul on the street."

Reb shook his head as he pulled a watch from his pocket. "Ain't likely to, either. It's nigh on ten o'clock. Ain't nobody up at this time of night."

"Except old moonshiners," J.D. concluded his friend's sentence.

"Never knew you to turn down a taste of my—"

J.D. held up a hand to silence Reb. The rider who had passed by only moments before now reined his horse toward the cantina again, approaching from the opposite direction. "Boys, I think this may be it."

This time the man below halted in front of the cantina, dismounted, and tied his horse to the hitching rail. As he walked inside, J.D. turned to his companions. "For a man looking for a good place to wash the trail dust from his throat, our friend down there gave the cantina the once-over five or ten times before coming in."

Footsteps on the stairs turned everyone's heads to the door. As Reb and Harlan cocked their shotguns once again, J.D. slipped his trusty Colt from its holster. He was beside the door when the knock came.

"McQuay? J.D. McQuay?"

J.D. frowned. How did the man outside know his name?

His unasked question was answered a moment later.

"The barkeep downstairs says you're in there, so open up. You and me, we got business to talk about," the man said.

J.D. unlocked the door and swung it wide. The man on the other side of the threshold stood tall, at eye level with him. Those eyes were as black as the hair poking out beneath a sweat-stained hat and the mustache drooping below the corners of his mouth. A sinister smile lifted one side of his mouth when he noticed the weapons held by the three men greeting him.

"I said I come to talk, not fight a war."

J.D. motioned for his companions to lower their

scatterguns. Reb and Harlan complied, although neither uncocked the hammers.

"You McQuay?" the man asked, his eyes focused on J.D.

"I'm J.D. McQuay. And you?"

"It don't make no never mind what my name is, McQuay. After tonight, ain't neither one of us ever goin' to see the other again."

J.D. watched the man's dark gaze dart about the room and alight on the stacked boxes of gold. He made no attempt to hide the recognition that lit up his face. "You said we had business to discuss."

"It's about your daughter, Katherine." The man reached into a back pocket and tugged out a wrinkled wad of green silk. "That's part of the dress she was wearin' when she was taken from the stage back in the Del Nortes."

J.D. unfolded the cloth. It was a jacket to a dress. "If this is supposed to assure me of something, it falls short. This could belong to any young lady."

The man sucked at his teeth with disgust and slipped a folded piece of paper from his shirt pocket. "Then maybe you'll know this."

Inside the folds was a lock of hair—auburn hair. J.D.'s eyes narrowed as he stared back icily at the messenger. "Where is she?"

"That's what I come to talk about," the man said. "If them boxes contain what I think they do, then you're to bring them to the old fort at straight up midnight. Your daughter will be there."

"The old fort?"

"Follow the river downstream about ten miles; you won't miss it. Just have the money there at midnight if you have any hopes of seeing your daughter again," the man said, and then turned and started to walk away.

"Now you wait just one durn minute," J.D. called to him.

The man looked back over his shoulder, frowning. "McQuay, I don't see how you could have any questions. I laid it out plain and simple-like."

"It's ten o'clock now," J.D. said. "It'll take an hour to get these boxes loaded onto the pack mules."

"That leaves you an hour to get to the fort. Time enough."

J.D. shook his head. "For a man alone on horseback, maybe. But not for men leading mules carrying gold. It'll take at least two hours to cover ten miles. And that will be pushing it."

The man's frown deepened. "You ain't tryin' to pull a fast one, are you, McQuay? 'Cause if you are, all it's goin' to get you is one dead daughter. You get my drift, don't you?"

"All I'm trying to do is assure that I have enough time to get the gold in those boxes to the fort," J.D. insisted.

The man bit at his lower lip and glared at J.D. for several moments. Wheels were turning inside his head. Eventually he nodded. "All right, McQuay. You got till one o'clock to get them boxes to the fort." He paused a moment before warning once again, "But don't go and try anythin' stupid. At the first sign of trouble, your daughter dies."

He did not wait for an answer this time, but turned his back on J.D. once again and walked hurriedly down the stairs. From the window, Harlan watched the man mount and ride away. "He headed east."

"Toward the old fort," Reb said.

"And we've got less than three hours to get the gold there." J.D. tugged his hat onto his head. "Reb, you and Harlan start moving the boxes downstairs. I'll leave General Lee here to help keep an eye on things while I go get the mules and horses."

J.D. left the room with his legs stretching in long, quick strides. Three hours was not much time, and he knew nothing about the old fort where Katherine was being held. A nasty situation had just taken a turn for the worse.

Chapter Fifteen

At eleven o'clock, after a sweaty hour's work, they double-checked the rifle, shotgun, and two revolvers each of them carried. J.D. watched as his two companions nodded that their weapons were loaded and ready. A tilt of his own head announced the time to move out had arrived.

Climbing into their saddles, J.D. and Reb each secured around their saddle horns the rope running back to the string of mules they led. Harlan fell back fifty feet behind the older men as they moved down Presidio's empty streets to reach the bank of the Rio Grande. There they reined to the left, heading downriver. J.D. signaled General Lee to take point, and the mongrel quickened his strides to move a hundred feet ahead of his human companions and their vulnerable cargo.

"In case I haven't mentioned it, I don't like the feel of this, J.D.," Reb said in a voice that was little more than a husky whisper. "I don't like it bein' the middle of the night, and I don't like it happenin' so far from town."

"It's not the way I'd choose, either," J.D. said. "But I'm not dealing the cards this hand."

Reb grunted. "That's somethin' else I don't like. We don't know who is dealin' cards. The only thing I'd give odds on is that whoever it is, he's usin' a marked deck."

His old friend had stated the obvious. The delivery of the ransom had been set in the old fort for one reason. J.D. suspected strongly that whoever waited there had no intention of letting either Katherine or the three of them live through this night. Nor had he ever intended to do so. If he had, the exchange would have taken place closer

143

to Monte Verde. Here, all the kidnappers had to do was
ride across the Rio Grande and they were beyond the
grasp of Texas lawmen.

Although Caitlyn had never said it, J.D. realized,
she, too, understood the desperation of the situation. If
she had not, she would never have sent for him. Nor
would she have given him free rein with the manner in
which he handled their daughter's return.

Caitlyn's image filled J.D.'s mind. He silently cursed—
not his wife, but himself. It had always been this way
when he rode toward danger. Thoughts of Caitlyn always
came into his head. Even during the war, before they had
married, he had seen her in his mind's eye before a battle.
Some men relived their lives at such times; he always
clung to thoughts of the person who was most dear to him.
His curses were because he had not had the sense to tell
Caitlyn exactly that back in Monte Verde, tell her how
empty his life had been without her, tell her how many
times in the past five years he had wanted to ride back and
attempt to set things straight between them.

But I was too pigheaded to swallow my pride. And
now, he might never have the chance to do so. He
promised himself that if he lived through this night, he
would tell Caitlyn everything.

He also knew he was lying to himself. It was a lie he
had told himself countless times during the years in New
Mexico. The moment he had seen Caitlyn back at the
ranch, saw that she was unchanged, his pride had swelled,
choking back the tender, conciliatory words he had wanted
to say for so long.

"Another thing I don't like"—Reb's voice wedged into
J.D.'s thoughts—"is this damned ride. A man could get
himself jumped a thousand times over in ten miles of trail
like this, passin' all them dark clumps of trees and bushes
along the river."

This thought had occurred to J.D. as well. Like it or
not, he had considered the possibility that Katherine was
no longer alive, that she had been killed shortly after she
was taken from the stage. The ride to the fort might be no
more than a ruse to lead them into an ambush. Which was
why he had sent the General ahead to sniff out the route.

The same reason kept his gaze constantly scanning the terrain they rode through.

"At least we'll have some light soon." Reb's head tilted toward the eastern horizon. "Moon's comin' up. Be much better if it was full."

The gibbous moon that pushed above the mountains to the east was five days past full. Its light had been enough for Comanche war parties to ride by back in Blood Moon times; it would be enough for the task they had ahead of them, J.D. thought.

General Lee came to an abrupt halt ahead. He growled at a copse of cottonwoods that grew near the river's edge.

J.D. threw up an arm, signaling a halt. As he slipped the Winchester from its saddle boot, Reb imitated his action and cocked his weapon with a single forward and back motion of his right arm.

Still growling, General Lee crept toward the clump of trees. He had covered half the distance when four deer, three doe and one buck, bounded from the cottonwoods and scampered toward the hills to the north.

An anxious breath, held overly long, escaped J.D.'s clenched teeth as the dog once more continued downriver. Lowering his shouldered rifle, J.D. nudged his mount forward again. "I thought—"

"The same thing I was a-thinkin'," Reb said. He also lowered his Winchester but followed J.D.'s example and kept the weapon out, balancing it in the crook of his left arm.

Behind them, Harlan followed the older men's lead and kept his own rifle ready. He tapped his mount's sides with his bootheels, moving the animal after his companions.

This ten-mile ride tonight, and the delivery of the ransom to an old fort that neither J.D. nor Reb knew anything about—this was not how Harlan had envisioned the exchange. In his mind he had expected the kidnappers to turn Katherine over in the streets of Presidio. Harlan now realized how naive that idea was—as naive, in fact, as his earlier notions about rescuing Katherine all by himself.

For the first time since leaving Monte Verde eight days earlier, he was fully cognizant of the danger that lay ahead. Neither J.D. nor Reb had said anything, but he could read it on their faces, feel it in their tension. The two men were expecting a fight to the finish when they got to the fort. They were prepared to kill the seven men who had kidnapped Katherine, or die trying.

The question that ate at his mind was—was he? To die trying did not bother him. He had always been willing to give all he had, even his life, for Katherine. It was the killing that gnawed at him.

The men who had attacked them in the desert had twisted something inside him. He had killed a man—a man he had thought of as a neighbor and a friend. As hard as he tried to push memories of that night from his mind, he could not. It haunted him; he had taken another man's life. That he had done so to protect himself and his comrades did not seem to matter. What did was that a human being's lifeblood had been spilled by his own hands. He did not ride any taller in the saddle because of this, but shorter, and sorrier, too.

Harlan closed his eyes and silently whispered a prayer for the strength he would need to see the night through.

Tate Lansdale rode briskly into the fort an hour after leaving Presidio. His men waited expectantly by a campfire.

"There's three of 'em," he announced. "And they'll be here at one."

"One?" Hank Yoakum asked. "I thought you set the time for midnight."

"There was a change in plans," Lansdale answered. "They ain't carryin' bank notes, and that's damn lucky for us. They brought gold—in little boxes, so they had to bring a whole train of mules with 'em."

"Gold!" That single word echoed among his men, brightening their long faces.

"Gold," Lansdale repeated. "No paper money, but gold that a man can spend anywhere."

Kelly Carter laughed out loud. "And in two more hours, it'll be all ours."

Lansdale let the smiles gradually fade from his men's faces. "It'll be ours if we're ready to take it. All of you know where you're supposed to be and what you have to do—so get to it."

As the men rose from the fire to take their strategic places about the fort, Lansdale reached out and grasped Ray Powell's shoulder. "Ray, I want you to stay right with the girl. If there's any trouble, put a bullet in her head."

Ray frowned. "You expectin' trouble?"

Doing his best to underplay the doubt he felt, Lansdale hiked his eyebrows and shrugged. "A man's always got to expect trouble."

"Right," Ray answered with an eager nod. "Don't worry about the girl. I said I'd handle her."

"Good. You're the kind of tough bastard I like havin' on my side." Lansdale smiled as he patted the man on the back. "I knew I could count on you."

As Ray walked to the shed to relieve Billy Crow of his guard duty, Lansdale squatted by the fire and poured himself a cup of coffee from the pot boiling on the flames. He had not expected to find J.D. McQuay himself in Presidio. From all accounts the man had left Texas for the New Mexico Territory years ago.

Not that McQuay changes anything, he told himself. McQuay was just another man. He and his two companions would die just fine, as would the girl. Then Lansdale would take care of the other five stooges standing between him and a millionaire's easy life in South America.

J.D. and Reb eased back on their reins, stopping an eighth of a mile from the first crumbling wall of the fort to come into view. A soft whistle called General Lee back to them, and a hand signal brought Harlan forward. The men huddled.

"Don't look like much, do it?" Reb stared at the ruins bathed in the soft moonlight.

"It looks tricky enough to get a man—or two or three—killed," J.D. said. "It has a bad feel to it, a real bad feel."

Harlan studied the older men and asked, "They don't intend to release Katherine, do they?"

J.D. turned to the young man. "I'm afraid that's the way I read it. If I were in their place, I would kill Katherine and all of us, then ride straight across the river into Mexico. They might surprise me and make the trade right out, but we can't play it that way and expect to come out of this thing alive."

A heavy silence fell over the three as their eyes returned to the fort. Reb eventually spoke. "A man can't see much from here. I sure as hell don't like us ridin' in there without doin' a little reconnoiterin' aforehand."

"Neither do I," J.D. replied. "That's why all of us aren't going inside. I'm riding in alone."

He waved away their protests before the two men could utter them, hastily explaining the seed of an idea that had taken root during the long ride from town.

Reb sucked at his tobacco-stained teeth when J.D. concluded, and then scratched his chin. "It ain't the smartest idea I ever heard, but it jist might work."

"That 'might' is all we have right now." J.D. untied the lead mule on his string, took the animal by its halter, and passed the remaining animals to Harlan. His gaze shifted between his two companions. "If you hear a shot, forget the gold. Come riding in with lead flying in front of you and get Katherine out of there."

When both Reb and Harlan nodded, J.D. looked down at General Lee. "Let's go, General."

He then tightened his right-handed hold on the single mule and moved forward, reins and cocked Winchester in his left hand. He realized the rifle would be all but impossible to swing into action if trouble broke out. But having it ready made him feel less vulnerable as he rode through the fort's entrance.

The deteriorating adobe walls enclosed what looked to J.D. in the blue moonlight like a full acre. While the majority of the buildings that had once stood within the walls were now no more than grass-covered mounds of earth, J.D. could count ten partially standing structures in various states of decay. The standing ruins roughly defined a broad avenue a hundred feet wide. Five of the structures rose on his left and four on the right. The tenth, a small boxlike building, stood at the end of the avenue near the south wall that fronted the Rio Grande.

The last of the buildings on his right was a long, low-slung structure faced with a line of doorless openings. A stable, J.D. surmised. It was there that the man who

had come to the cantina stood beside the flickering flames
of a campfire. He was by himself, sipping at a cup of coffee
and holding a rifle in his right hand.

The rifle and cup were of little interest to J.D. The
fact that he was alone was. One man did not add up to the
seven who had taken Katherine from the stage. J.D.'s eyes
darted from one side of the avenue to the other, probing
the ruins and the shadows they cast. He knew the remaining
six men must be hiding among the structures, but he
could not fathom how they might be deployed.

General Lee, however, did. And if the dog did not
actually see the men, he caught their scent. A growl rose
in his throat as he passed the third building on the right.
Similar growls pinpointed men concealed in the second
and third structures on the left side of the avenue and a
fourth hidden in a building directly across from the stable.

Quick ciphering brought the tally of four men in the
buildings and one by the fire to a total of five. Worried
furrows wrinkled J.D.'s brow. Two of the kidnappers remained
unaccounted for. Neither his eyes nor General Lee's nose
had located them.

The man standing near the campfire took a pocket
watch from his breeches and opened it as J.D. approached
him. "One o'clock on the dot, McQuay. You're a punctual
man."

"You didn't give me much choice." J.D. drew his
mount to a halt ten feet from the man. His eyes ran again
along the doorless stalls. Were the other two men hidden
in this building?

"I also told you not to try anythin' stupid, McQuay."
The man tossed out his remaining coffee and dropped the
tin cup to the ground. "What is this? There ain't one mule
in this whole world that could carry half a million in gold
on his back."

J.D. shrugged. "Let's call it insurance, or a down
payment, if you like. The rest of the gold's outside. As
soon as I see that my daughter's alive and unharmed, I'll
go out and signal my men to bring it in."

"This ain't the way I told you," Lansdale said
threateningly. He frowned, his dark eyes glaring up at
J.D.

"But that's the way it is." J.D.'s tone left no room for bargaining. "When I see my daughter, you get the rest of the money."

The man stroked his drooping mustache for several seconds. He had not anticipated such bravado from a man whose daughter was still captive. Finally he agreed to the conditions. "Before you see your daughter, though, I see the color of your money."

"Fair enough. The keys to the locks are in my shirt pocket."

"Dig 'em out slow and easy-like."

Balancing the Winchester in his lap, J.D. used two fingers to bring a ring of keys from his pocket. He leaned back, unlocked the two boxes on the mule's back, and flipped open the lids. "There are sixteen more boxes like this outside."

The man walked up to the mule and plunged a hand into one of the small chests and then into the other. A pleased smile spread across his face as he examined the golden coins that trickled musically between his fingers. His eyes rose to J.D. again. "I like the color of your money, McQuay. I like it a lot." He then called toward the shack near the south wall. "Ray, bring the girl out here. I got a man who wants to take a look at her."

A sixth man used the muzzle of a rifle to poke Katherine from the shed to the campfire. A knot twisted and doubled itself in J.D.'s gut. In spite of the five years that had passed since he had last seen her, the men's clothing she wore, her disarrayed hair, and the dirt that smudged her right cheek, this was undoubtedly his daughter. He saw glimpses of himself in the face that uplifted to him, but there was no mistaking the delicate features and beauty she had inherited from Caitlyn.

The light of recognition sparked in her green eyes as she stared up at him. Yet she said nothing.

Ignoring the ache in his chest and the racing beat of his heart, J.D. suppressed the urge to spur his mount forward, sweep Katherine up into the saddle, and ride hell-bent for leather from this place of decay. He had come to rescue his daughter, not to get both of them killed.

"All right, McQuay, you've had your eyeful. She's

alive and nobody's hurt her." Slamming shut the lids to the boxes, the man took the mule from J.D. "Now go bring the rest of the gold in here."

Allowing himself another glance at Katherine, J.D. called to General Lee, reined his horse about, and rode back down the avenue separating the crumbling buildings. General Lee's growls reconfirmed the locations of the four men hidden behind those decaying adobe walls. And still, J.D. could only account for six of the seven men who had kidnapped his daughter. Where was the seventh?

Placing six out of seven men cut the advantage the kidnappers had held before he rode in, he told himself. But he could not shake the feeling that the seventh man would suddenly appear and shatter the plan that formed in his mind. Like it or not, there was nothing he could do about that seventh man. He had been dealt a hand; the time had come to play his cards.

Chapter Sixteen

"You saw her? And she's all right?" Harlan asked anxiously. "She hasn't been hurt?"

"She looks a little mussed up, but she's okay." J.D. glanced at the young man out of the corner of an eye. That something he detected in Harlan's voice whenever he spoke of Katherine was there again. Did something exist between his daughter and this deputy that he was unaware of? J.D. shoved the thought aside. A lot of things could have happened in five years that he would not know about. And none of them had any bearing on what now had to be done here tonight.

Squatting on his heels, he used a fingertip to draw a rough outline of the fort in the sand. He added ten squares within and placed an X on four of the squares. "This is where the General sniffed out men. The other two are here by the stable with Katherine. I'll take them myself. The four hidden in the buildings are yours."

"That only adds up to six men." Harlan stared at J.D. "Seven men hit the stage."

"Yeah, I know. But these six were all I could locate," J.D. said. "We'll have to worry about the seventh man when he shows himself." He looked at the old scout. "Reb, do you see anything I missed?"

Reb shook his head. "I ain't as fast as I once was and I'd rather be on horseback, but I don't see no other way but to go in on foot."

"The mules will give you the only cover you have," J.D. explained. "You two would be sitting ducks on horses."

"Like you'll be." Reb's head turned to his friend.

"Don't worry about this duck. Just take care of the two on the right." J.D. stood. "Now let's sort out those ropes and packs. I want all hell to break loose in there with the first shot."

Drawing hunting knives, the three men worked their way down the lines of mules. Steel sliced into hemp, leaving only a few strands of the rope to bind each of the pack animals. As quickly as their fingers could work, they loosened the packs on each mule. There was no time to double-check their efforts.

J.D. climbed into the saddle. Taking each lead rope, he gave them one loop around his saddle horn. A single tug would loosen them and free him of the mules, the mules of him. Reins in left hand and cocked rifle in right, he looked behind him. Reb and Harlan, rifles ready, stood in between the two strings of mules. Both were stooped slightly in an attempt to hide as much of themselves as possible behind the gold-bearing animals.

"We have to move out. I don't want the men in the fort getting too impatient," J.D. said.

"We're as ready as we'll ever be." Reb waved his friend forward.

With General Lee ahead, a string of mules to each side of him, and two men behind, J.D. tapped his mount's sides and rode toward a rendezvous with some kind of destiny. Reaching the entrance, he saw the two men by the fire, standing with his daughter. His finger slipped around the rifle trigger and rested there. Drawing a breath to quell the hammering of his heart, he headed straight down the avenue separating the lines of ruins. There was no turning back now; he was committed to seeing this through to the end.

J.D.'s eyes focused on the two men with Katherine, watching each for a gesture or a nod of the head that would signal the others to open fire. He tried not to think about the four gunmen hidden in the buildings he passed or the whereabouts of the unknown seventh man. For now, those were Reb and Harlan's concerns. The two men ahead were his, and he had to take them if Katherine was to live.

A smile spread across the face of the man who had

come to the room in Presidio as J.D. approached. His
hungry eyes caressed the strings of gold-laden mules.

Half a dozen strides from the man, J.D. halted. He
unlooped the ropes from the saddle horn and let them fall
to the ground. "Here's the gold. Now I'll take my daughter and be on my way."

"That ain't very neighborly of you, McQuay. To ride
all this way and not even stay around for a visit." The man
edged away from the fire as though angling for a better
position when the fighting started. "But you ain't goin'
nowhere until I check out each and every one of these
boxes."

The man stopped suddenly when General Lee turned
to face him with a feral snarl that exposed long, unfriendly
teeth.

"Let my daughter go; then you can check the chests."
J.D. watched the one called Ray out of the corner of his
eye. The man still held Katherine at gunpoint.

"You know I can't do that, McQuay." The mustached
man tried to take another step, but stopped once again
when General Lee crept forward, a low growl rumbling in
his throat. "Ray, you know what to do with the girl.
There's no need wastin'—"

J.D. did not wait for him to finish his sentence.
Instead he shouted, "Katherine, get down!"

As his daughter threw herself to the ground, J.D.
snapped the Winchester up. Holding it at arm's length
like a revolver, he aimed straight for Ray's chest and fired.

In the next instant the hell he had wanted broke
loose!

Harlan saw J.D.'s rifle whip up and heard the shot. A
heartbeat later, the mules panicked. Braying and bucking
under their huge weight, they lunged eight different
directions at once. The partly severed ropes that held
them snapped. The animals went wild in their freedom.
Their braying doubled as they ran, kicking and tumbling.
One by one the boxes of gold that had been strapped to
their backs flew through the air. A ringing shower of shiny,
slippery gold coins spilled out on the ground.

"Move it, boy!" Harlan heard Reb shout behind him.
He glanced over his shoulder. The older man was

halfway to the nearest structure on the right. Rifle held waist-high, he scrambled beside one of the loose mules, using it for cover.

Remembering his own task, Harlan came alive and darted toward a half-collapsed adobe building on the left. Somewhere to his back, he heard the bark of four more rifle shots. Then several cries of "The gold! The gold! Get the gold!" rose around him. He ignored everything and kept running.

"The damn mules are spillin' the gold!" A man burst from around a ragged wall directly in front of Harlan. "We got to get the gold 'fore them mules scatter it from here to king—"

The man skidded to a halt as though noticing Harlan for the first time. Harlan's rifle rose, barrel homing on the man's chest. His finger curled around the trigger.

He hesitated. Images of the townsfolk he had left behind in the desert flashed before his mind's eye.

The gunman in front of him did not hesitate. His rifle snapped up. Yellow and blue flames leapt from the muzzle.

A fiery hot brand sliced across Harlan's left forearm. Pain instantly dissipated the ghosts haunting his mind. Reality, hard and cruel, rocked through him. He could either fight or throw his own life away. He chose life. His finger squeezed down on the trigger.

The impact of the slug threw the gunman back against the adobe wall. With a grunt, he slid to the ground—obviously dead.

To his right, Harlan saw a dark shape dart from the shadows cast by the second structure he had been assigned to cover. That shape held a rifle in its hand, which it swung toward him.

Throwing himself to the ground, he ducked beneath the angry metallic hornet that screamed through the air above his head. Again he lifted his rifle, aimed, and fired.

The man staggered back as the bullet slammed into him. Somehow managing to keep his legs beneath him, he swayed drunkenly as he lifted his rifle again.

Harlan fired once more. This time the man seemed to implode, and he fell, never to rise again.

Reb snatched at the mule's halter, two fingers locking

around the leather. He clung to the animal, letting it pull him along as it ran toward the first of the buildings he meant to clean out. Lead whined hot and angry over the mule's back as a man stepped into a jagged hole that had once been a window and proceeded to open fire with a six-gun.

Holding dearly to the mule, Reb counted each shot that blasted from the barrel. When the sixth report thundered, he released the halter, let the mule run by, shouldered his rifle, and fired.

The gunman died with a cry of surprise on his lips as he struggled to reload, never getting past emptying the spent shells from his weapon.

Three strides brought Reb to the building's wall. He threw his back against it and looked to the right—and cursed. He could no longer see J.D. or Katherine. The liberated mules were everywhere, braying and bucking in their fear like wild mustangs.

His gaze jumped across the now-empty avenue and saw Harlan take down a man who ran from one of the structures. Assured the young man was holding his own, Reb looked at the crumbling ruins that stood on his left.

A rifleman stepped through a gaping hole in the wall. He shouldered his weapon and aimed across the avenue, taking a sure bead on Harlan.

There was no time for a carefully aimed shot. Pumping the Winchester's lever like a madman, Reb fired six frantic rounds in rapid succession. He was certain the second shot struck the kidnapper, but the man did not hit the ground until the sixth shot tore into his body, too, as a coup de grace.

At the instant J.D. had first squeezed the rifle trigger to set the men in motion, General Lee had leapt for the mustached kidnapper. J.D. heard two cries, but saw neither of their sources. He was too busy trying to scramble off the back of his falling horse.

Two of the freed mules had run head-on into the horse. Nostrils flaring, neighing in wild-eyed panic, the animal reared—too high. As it lost balance, it began to tumble backward.

Kicking free of the stirrups, J.D. threw himself from

the saddle. He hit the ground in an awkward roll as the echo of gunshots ricocheted off the walls of the old fort. Struggling to get his legs under him, he stood. He focused first on the campfire.

The kidnapper named Ray lay stretched facedown in the sand. He did not move.

Beside him, Katherine pushed up on her elbows.

"Stay down!" J.D. shouted, waving his daughter back to a safer level. "Get down and stay down until Reb or I tell you to get up."

Katherine's eyes found him. She immediately dropped back to her stomach, covering her head.

He had lost his rifle when he had leapt from his horse. J.D. wrenched the Colt lightning-fast from its holster and pivoted to face the mustached kidnapper.

The man was nowhere to be seen, but his rifle now lay on the ground. Beside it was General Lee. The dog was motionless, blood trickling from his head.

Cursing, J.D. scanned the fort. The mules, each trying to run in three directions at once, eliminated even a hope of glimpsing how Reb and Harlan had fared. Nor did he catch sight of the mysterious missing gunman.

Wait! A blur of movement to his left swung J.D. around. The man he sought moved with labored steps toward the southern wall of the fort. In his arms was one of the boxes of gold. It did not take a genius to realize that the man had seen the tables turn and decided to abandon his companions, taking a share of the gold as he went.

Raising the Colt, J.D. fired at the fleeing man. A little puff of dust billowed at the kidnapper's feet as the shot fell short.

Apparently recognizing the danger, the man tossed aside the chest and ran. The box burst open, and hundreds of coins spilled on the ground.

J.D. gave chase. Twice more he fired, and twice more his shots went wild, burying themselves in the dirt. With a string of curses bursting from his lips, he watched the man vault over a low section of the wall and run toward the river.

Doubling his own speed, J.D. reached the wall. Coming to a dead stop, he sucked in a steadying breath, lifted the Colt, and aimed. As he exhaled, he squeezed the trigger.

This time he found his mark. The fleeing kidnapper went rigid as the bullet struck. Then he fell facedown in the Rio Grande. His body jerked and twitched as the current slowly swept it downstream.

Lowering the revolver, J.D. was suddenly aware of the silence that surrounded him. He swung around, startled by the conspicuous absence of gunshots. He found Reb and Harlan standing by the fire with a shaken but happy Katherine.

"Get him?" Reb called out.

"Got him." J.D. returned the Colt to its holster.

"Then that's it," Reb said with a satisfied grin. "This moonlight party is over."

J.D. smiled. It was over. But it hadn't been any goldarn "party." His long nightmare was finally done.

Chapter Seventeen

"**S**it down by the fire and be still," Katherine demanded. "I want to take a look at that arm. You've been wounded, in case you were too busy to notice."

Harlan glanced down at the blood-soaked sleeve of his shirt. "I've noticed, all right. This is burning like all get-out."

"Then why don't you sit down and let me see how bad it is?" Katherine said.

"It's not bad," Harlan assured her, but he settled by the campfire just the same. "I should be helping your pa and ol' Reb gather in the mules and load up the scattered gold."

Taking the knife from the sheath on his belt, Katherine used the blade to open his shirtsleeve. "Both of them are grown men and quite capable of tending stock. Besides, neither one of them is wounded." She gasped as she exposed his wound. "Look at this! You might have been killed!"

"We all might have been killed. But a little scratch like that isn't about to do a man in." J.D. pulled a leather pouch from his saddlebag and tossed it to his daughter. "There's sulfur and bandaging inside. I carry it in case I have to do some horse doctoring. But if you wash his arm, sprinkle on some of that sulfur, and wrap the wound loosely with the bandaging, I suspect he'll live."

"That's loosely," Reb added with a chuckle of obvious delight. "Don't want to go and get it too tight or gangrene will set in and rot that arm right up to the shoulder."

Katherine ignored both men, although she accepted a canteen Reb handed her and began washing Harlan's arm.

J.D. watched his daughter for several seconds before motioning Reb back to the gold waiting to be loaded on

159

the mules. The old scout came toward J.D. with a wink and an ear-to-ear grin. "Looks like you lost out by not gettin' yourself shot up. That young'un of yours hasn't stopped lookin' at that young buck for the last hour and a half."

J.D. glanced back at Katherine and Harlan, and then lifted one of the boxes to a mule and strapped it down securely. "Believe me, I've noticed."

"Seems with you bein' her father and all, you'd at least rate a hug and peck on the cheek," Reb continued. "But she don't even give you a thank-you."

"Old man, have I ever said that you talk too much?"

"Oh, I'm sure you have, but I didn't pay it any more mind than I do most else what you say."

J.D. caught his eyes wandering back to Katherine. In spite of himself, he felt a twinge of jealousy over the attention Harlan received. Katherine had not said half a dozen words to him, nor had she called him by name. Five years had put more distance between his daughter and himself than he had realized.

Yet, what else could he expect? When he had left for New Mexico, she had been a vulnerable child of thirteen. Now she was a young lady. For all he knew, he might be no more to her these days than a vague recollection of someone she used to call "Daddy." The good Lord knew this full-grown woman was not the young girl he remembered.

"You know, we were damned lucky, J.D." Reb tightened a leather strap around another chest. "Those men could just as easily have cut us down as been killed themselves— 'specially if the seventh man had been with 'em."

J.D. nodded. "But they didn't, and we survived. That's what matters."

He would have liked to believe that simply because he and his companions had right on their side, they had overcome the six men. But he was not that naive. Lady Luck, as Reb had said, plus eight braying and kicking mules, had more to do with the results than anything else.

"One man with a grazed arm and a dog with a goose egg on his head." Reb winked at his friend. "Yep, I'd say we were damned lucky and then some."

J.D.'s eyes shifted to the fire again. General Lee sat

resting by the flames. The mongrel looked a little dazed, and dried blood matted the hair on the right side of his head, but the dog was a long way from dying.

He could only guess at what had happened when General Lee went for Lansdale, having himself been occupied with keeping from being crushed under his own horse at the time. However, because of the rifle he had found beside the unconscious dog, he imagined Lansdale had defended himself from the attack by using the weapon as a bludgeon rather than firing it. He had merely knocked General Lee unconscious, though J.D. was certain Lansdale's intentions had been otherwise.

"See?" Harlan held his cleansed forearm in the firelight so Katherine could examine it. "It weren't much more than a scratch."

She gave him a sidelong glance as she sprinkled sulfur powder onto the wound and began to bandage it. "It could have been worse. You wouldn't have known without looking at it."

Harlan offered no argument. Instead, he sat back and drank in the sight of the beautiful young girl, grateful for the attention she lavished on him.

Nor did his penetrating looks go unnoticed, or unappreciated. Katherine studied his face from the corner of an eye while she worked. She had always thought of Harlan as handsome, but never quite as handsome as he was at this moment, in the firelight and in the afterglow of victory. To be certain, the cut of his clothes was not exactly the current style in Austin and Houston, nor was the trim of his hair. But even her mother had warned her time and again that clothes do not make a man.

Man. Her thoughts stumbled on the word. She recalled each of the men she had met this past year; *men*, but she did not think of them as such. In her mind they were all overgrown boys, each awaiting the time, if it ever came, to prove himself a man.

Harlan, she realized, had always been a man. For all the years she had known him, she had never thought of him as a boy. Perhaps it was because he was three years older than she. She nibbled at her lower lip. That thought rang hollow and false. Harlan had always been a man...

because he was a man. The neat circularity of her feelings escaped Katherine. All she knew was that Harlan did not have to prove himself. He knew what he wanted, and he went after it, whatever it was. She admired him.

And he had always been there for her. Even as a child, it was Harlan she had turned to with whispered schoolgirl confidences or requests to retrieve pecans from tree branches too high for her to climb.

And he was always there. The thought jarred her mind. How many years had she looked at this young man in the light of day and never seen the way of it? It took a campfire and all this terrible shooting to open her eyes and make her recognize the truth—about Harlan, about herself. That something she had felt missing in the young men she had met during the past year was sitting right here in front of her.

Without the slightest warning, she turned and stared at Harlan eye to eye. "Harlan Brewster, you're in love with me, aren't you?"

Not even an eye batted when he answered, "Yes."

"That's good." She leaned forward and lightly kissed his lips. A smile lit her face when they parted. "That's real good."

Reb chuckled when he noticed the kiss out of the corner of his eye. He shot a glance at J.D. but could not tell if his friend had caught the display of affection between the two youngsters. If he had, J.D. was not reacting like any father he had ever met. "Looks like Katherine has found herself a real hero."

A frown knitted J.D.'s brow, but he made no comment, except to say, "That's the last of the boxes. Now all we have to do is hope the knots in these ropes hold until we get back to Presidio. The last thing I want is to chase mules by moonlight over half of Texas."

Giving the two strings of pack animals one last check, he announced, "It's ten miles back to town. If we're going to beat the sun, we'd better be moving out."

"What about the stock Lansdale and his men were ridin'?" Reb's eyes widened with interest.

"I've no use for them," J.D. answered. "Do with them as you please."

Rubbing his hands together, Reb called to Harlan, "Get up off your backside, boy, and help gather them horses. We're lookin' at a major bonanza. With the five head we picked up out on the trail, and these, too, I'm gonna have enough to start my own horse ranch!"

As the two men hastened to gather the outlaws' horses and mule from the decaying stable, J.D. watched Katherine rise from the fire and walk to him. "Are you all right?" he asked when she returned the leather pouch containing the sulfur and bandages. He thought that by now the shock of being rescued and the impact of so much violent, bloody death around her might have made her faint or cry.

Her eyes rolled to the ground, as her gaze refused to meet his. "I'm doing as well as can be expected, I guess. And I'm doing a lot better than I expected." She studied the horses for a moment. "Which one am I supposed to ride?"

J.D. felt a father's love swell to the point of bursting within his chest. He wanted to take this young woman in his arms and hug her tightly, to tell her that it was over, that everything would be all right. But Katherine gave no indication she wanted or needed that kind of assurance from him. As far as he could tell, she did not even want to talk with him. So he said, businesslike, "Take the bay back there. Harlan was riding it, but he can use one of the horses he's bringing from the stable."

Katherine nodded and, without uttering another word, walked to the horse and mounted.

Suppressing the urge to shake his head, J.D. turned to the fire and lifted General Lee into his arms. He placed the injured dog across his saddle and then climbed up behind him. General Lee, resting partially on the saddle and partially on J.D.'s legs, lifted his head and gave his owner a questioning, if somewhat blurry-eyed, look.

J.D. reached down and gently patted the animal's shoulder. "Relax and enjoy the ride. You earned it tonight."

When Reb and Harlan swung astride their mounts, J.D. reined his horse about and headed from the fort, never glancing at the bodies of the five dead men they left behind.

*   *   *

Tate Lansdale's lungs burned in his chest like the fires of hell. Still he held his breath as he floated along, motionless and facedown in the water, letting the current sweep him away from the certain death that waited upstream on the riverbank behind him.

A minute, two, three, seared by as the scalding flames built in his lungs and flared out, spreading from his chest down his arms and legs. Unable to contain his air-starved body any longer, he jerked his head from the water. His mouth opened wide, and he sucked down the cool night air to pull himself back from the slippery edge of unconsciousness.

Then he froze, heart pounding in a runaway tempo, as he waited for the bark of a six-gun and the burning lead that would surely tear into his back.

Neither came.

Slowly, cautiously, he twisted in the water, wincing when pain shot through his left shoulder. The anguish slowly left his face and was replaced by a pleased smile when he stared upriver. The fort and J.D. McQuay were no longer in sight. The water had carried him around a bend in the river—and far beyond gun range.

Lansdale twisted again, preparing to swim toward the bank. His boots touched the river's rocky bottom. With little effort, he managed to get his feet under him and stand. The water came only to his waist. As quickly as he could, he scrabbled out of the water and dropped beside the twisted trunk of an ancient mesquite tree.

His head cocked from side to side as he listened for approaching footsteps. When he was certain there were none, he opened his shirt and eased back the collar. Another smile touched his lips. McQuay had hit him all right, but the bullet had only nicked his left shoulder.

Leaning against the mesquite trunk, Lansdale smiled. He was still alive. And although J.D. McQuay did not know it yet, this simple fact meant that McQuay was a dead man.

Chapter Eighteen

J.D. felt good—tired, but good—as he stepped from a steaming bath, toweled himself dry, and slipped into the new shirt and breeches he had bought at one of Presidio's two general stores. The McQuay fortune, transmuted to boxes of gold coins, was safely locked away in one of Carlos Tinajas's jail cells, with four men guarding them around the clock. The horses and mules were in the livery stable, grained, hayed, and bedded down. General Lee was there, too, gnawing on the biggest beef bone J.D. could find in town.

Now all that remains is to fill my own stomach and maybe catch a few winks. When the telegraph office opened later in the afternoon, Katherine and he would wire a message to Caitlyn. She would be enormously relieved. He refused to think about the long ride back to the Circle Q that would begin at daybreak tomorrow. Today, he planned to enjoy himself and rest. He had earned that, and so had the others.

He ran a hand over his clean-shaven cheeks as he examined himself in a mirror that hung on the bathhouse wall. He looked none the worse for the wear. Considering that the odds were two to one that he should have died last night, he regarded that as something of a minor miracle.

Harlan was waiting for him behind the barbershop when he stepped from the bathhouse. The boy, dressed in the new duds J.D. had bought for him, appeared as nervous as a long-tailed cat in a room full of rocking chairs.

"Mr. McQuay, I need to have a word with you in

private." Harlan twisted the brim of the hat he held in his hands.

"I think after what we've been through, you can call me J.D.—or Mac, the way your pa did. I'd like that," J.D. said.

"I'll stick with 'Mr. McQuay' until you've heard what I have to say, sir." Harlan swallowed hard and looked to him nervously for a signal to proceed.

J.D.'s eyes narrowed. "You're giving me the distinct feeling that I'm not going to like what I hear, but I'm listening."

Harlan swallowed hard again. "I come for your permission to court your daughter, Katherine."

"From that kiss I saw last night, I don't think you need my permission." J.D. laughed. "But for what it's worth, you have my permission. And I wish you good luck when you have this same little talk with Katherine's mother."

The smile that had just blossomed on Harlan's face was transformed instantly into a mask of pale ash.

"Hadn't given Caitlyn a thought, had you, son?" J.D. waved the young man through the rear door of the barbershop ahead of him. "Well, here's the only word of advice I'll ever give you about getting involved with this family— don't ever forget about Caitlyn Marie Kennedy McQuay, or you'll rue the day you did."

"Yes, sir, I see your point," Harlan answered with a firm nod of his head.

Inside, Reb waited for them. It took a long, hard look for J.D. to recognize his old friend. With his crisp-looking new store-bought clothes and a haircut and shave, he appeared ten years younger than the man who had walked in here for tonsorial service an hour ago.

"What do y'all say to heading back to our rooms, picking up Katherine, and finding us some steak and eggs for breakfast?" J.D. suggested.

Reb opened the barbershop door for his companions. "I'd say all we have to do is step outside and wait a couple of minutes. I just saw Katherine up the street a piece, comin' our way." He looked at Harlan and winked. "She was wearin' that new green dress J.D. bought her and looked as pretty as a sunrise over the Del Norte Mountains."

J.D. followed Reb's suggestion and walked outside.

His chest swelled with pride when his gaze alighted on the young woman two blocks away hastening toward them. Katherine was blossoming into a woman as beautiful as her mother. Caitlyn had done a fine job of raising the girl to carry herself with such finesse and grace.

And she was a young woman with a head on her shoulders, he thought. Katherine could have done a lot worse than finding a solid, sensitive man like Harlan Brewster.

"McQuay! J.D. McQuay!"

J.D. turned casually and faced four dusty mounted men who reined their horses to a halt in the middle of the street. He recognized the oldest of the four; he had never seen the three younger men at his side. "Bill Wayne, isn't it? Well, howdy. You've got a spread north of Monte Verde, I believe."

"That's right, McQuay. And these are my sons." He nodded to the men beside him. "We was supposed to meet up with my brother Russell on the way down here. We found him layin' in a grave four days back."

Harlan stepped just behind J.D. and whispered quickly, "Russell Wayne was with the five men who attacked us by the arroyo."

J.D. needed no more explanation to know that these four were the second group of desperadoes who had followed them all the way from the Circle Q. In all likelihood, they had wasted a couple of days following Caitlyn's decoy before deciding to join the men who had attacked in the desert.

Before J.D. could answer Wayne, Harlan stepped forward. "Mr. Wayne, what happened to your brother and those other men couldn't be helped. They came gunning for us. They were after the—"

"Deputy, I knowed what they was after," Wayne said. "The same thing we come to get. And mean to have."

In the space of a heartbeat, Wayne yanked a pistol from the holster strapped on his hip, raised it, and fired straight at Harlan.

J.D.'s right hand dropped for his Colt the instant he saw Wayne start to make a move. He was not fast enough to stop the man from firing, but his own shot struck Wayne in the forehead the moment the man's pistol barked.

J.D. saw Harlan's legs crumple under him. There was no time to see to the young man—not now. J.D.'s Colt was already swinging to the right.

Wayne's three sons awkwardly wrenched their own pistols free, as surprised by their father's impetuous move as by his bloody demise. They fired, not at Harlan, but at the man who had shot their father.

Hot lead whistled past J.D.'s own head to whine off the adobe building behind him. He neither flinched nor blinked. Two more times he pulled the trigger. There was no need for a third. Beside him Reb fired two quick rounds at the Wayne brothers, and all three fell off their horses, dead weight hitting the ground.

"Harlan! Harlan!" Katherine ran across the street, tears streaming down her cheeks. She dropped to her knees beside the young man.

"I'm okay." Harlan lifted his head. "He just hit me in the shoulder. I'll live."

"That boy better take a mite more care with that left arm." Reb slipped his pistol back into its holster. "He's gonna get the damned thing shot off if he don't watch hisself."

J.D. was dumbstruck by this latest round of gunfighting. He paid no attention to his friend's dark humor. Instead he glanced at Harlan to make certain the gunshot wound was no worse than the young man said. Wayne had hit him in the shoulder, and he did not appear to be bleeding that much. J.D. turned to Reb. "Hurry and get Tinajas, tell him what happened, then get a doctor for Harlan. I'll see about those four."

As Reb ran toward the sheriff's office, J.D., the hot metal of his Colt still in hand, stepped toward the four men in the street. None of them moved, but he had seen more than one man die from a bullet in the back fired by a wounded enemy playing possum.

It took but one glance at Bill Wayne to confirm what J.D. already knew; the man was dead. So were his three sons, but J.D. had to roll two of them on their backs to make certain. He closed his eyes and silently cursed what lust for money could do. Because of the greed of a few crazed men, so many had died.

"Are they all dead?" Harlan called to him.

J.D. turned. "Yep, all of them. I—"

The thunder of a firing rifle cracked the air behind him.

A sledgehammer slammed into J.D.'s right shoulder. He cried out as the force of the impact threw him face-down in the street. *What? How?* He tried to find answers to the questions that were spinning through his head, but could not fight past the burning brand of white-hot pain that seared deep within his shoulder.

"How's that feel, McQuay, you son of a bitch? I hope it hurts like hell!"

Panic squeezed like an iron band around J.D.'s chest. He knew that voice! But it had to be a voice come back like Lazarus from the dead. It belonged to Tate Lansdale!

Shifting just enough to glance down the street, he saw Lansdale swaggering toward him. The man grimaced as he cocked the rifle he held in both hands. J.D.'s left arm shot out, his fingers searching for the Colt he had lost when he fell. All his hand closed around was sand. He never took his eyes off Lansdale.

"I wish I could watch you hurt all day, McQuay. Would be a pleasure, yes indeed. But I ain't got the time. Me and that daughter of yours are goin' to collect us half a million in gold, then we're gonna take us a l'il trip down south of the border." Lansdale hiked the rifle to his shoulder and aimed. "But first, I'm going to see you past the pearly gates!"

A gun barked! It was not Lansdale's!

J.D. blinked. He saw but did not comprehend what was happening.

Lansdale staggered backward. The rifle flew up from his hands and exploded by itself when it hit the street. He stared down at the weapon. Shaking in fear and astonishment, his head lifted; disbelief washed over his face. His right hand rose to his chest. When it came away, blood was smeared across his palm. He looked about him for an explanation and seemed to find none; then his legs slowly gave way beneath him and he collapsed to the street.

J.D.'s eyes shifted from the dead outlaw. Katherine was kneeling beside Harlan with the deputy's still smoking revolver in her hands. Her look darted from Lansdale to J.D.

"Father!" She threw the gun aside and pushed to her feet. "Father!" The call was choked with tears and outrage.

She ran to him, dropped beside him, and wrapped her arms around him. Something had broken inside her, a dam of reserve, fear, and bitterness, which was now swept away. She clung to him. "Father!" she repeated, sobbing, unable to say more.

"I'm still alive," he moaned as he rolled over. "But I don't know if I cotton to that 'Father' of yours. You used to call me Daddy."

In spite of the tears spilling down her cheeks, she managed to smile. "I still do, if that's what you like."

"I like it, and I love you, Katherine." He encircled her with his left arm and drew her to him again.

"Damn!" Reb cursed somewhere above him. "I go and leave you for a few minutes, and all you can do is go and get yourself shot! Bejeezus, you're a tough man to work for."

J.D. was not given the opportunity to answer. Katherine looked up at the old scout. "Where's that doctor you were sent to get?"

Reb blinked and stepped back. The surprised expression on his face told J.D. that his friend had heard the same thing in Katherine's tone that J.D. had—the authority of a Caitlyn!

"There ain't no sawbones in Presidio." Reb eventually found his voice. "But there's one across the river in Ojinaga. The sheriff's gone to fetch him."

"Well, don't just stand there with your mouth gaping." Katherine pointed to the crowd that gathered around. "Get some of these men to help me carry Harlan and my fath—daddy to their rooms. A dirty street is no place for wounded men."

"Yes, ma'am." Reb snapped into action.

Senator Throckmorton walked from the guest room to the gallery that stretched along the back of the Big House.

His gaze found Caitlyn seated at a table in the morning sun. "Good morning, my dear. You look lovely with the sunlight striking your hair that way."

"Thank you, Herschel." Caitlyn motioned for the man to join her at the table, wishing she had taken breakfast in the solitude of her bedroom this morning.

However, she refused to allow a blowhard like Herschel Throckmorton to cheat her out of watching the morning sun transform the prairie dew into millions of sparkling diamonds. The morning ritual had begun more years ago than she liked to remember. Then there had been no servants to prepare her breakfast, and no Big House. J.D. and she had simply shared a cup of coffee on their front stoop and watched the sun rise together.

"I've looked in on Clay," Throckmorton said. "He's feeling much better today. I believe he'll come downstairs later on."

"I'm delighted to hear that," Caitlyn answered in her sweetest voice.

In truth, she was more than ready for Clay Throckmorton to be strong enough to walk out the front door and take his father with him. The man had been on the Circle Q for a week now, and she would be happy never to see him again in her life. She had forgotten how boring such men could be as a steady diet. During her short visits to Austin, those of Senator Throckmorton's ilk always appeared so charming and sophisticated. But then, she only saw them in their best light, at parties and social functions. Men like Herschel Throckmorton were born to shine on such occasions.

However, after a week of the senator's almost constant companionship, she recalled how tedious they really were. As a girl in Austin, she had known that. It was one of the reasons she had first been attracted to J.D. Cocksure of himself he might have been, and a bit unpolished, but there was sincerity in his voice and eyes—and dreams in his words.

Caitlyn smiled. When J.D. spoke, she mused, *I* was not every other word he used.

"I swear, Caitlyn, I really don't understand why you persist in living way out here on the edge of nowhere."

Throckmorton poured himself a cup of coffee from the china pot on the table bedecked with fresh flowers and a fine lace tablecloth. He glanced at her as he stirred in three teaspoons of sugar and a healthy portion of cream. "It really is a barren wasteland."

Caitlyn gazed over the blue-green prairie. The sunlight was caught in each drop of morning dew. How many times had she watched this marvel of life and never grown tired of it? Each day it was like a new miracle for her.

"My father was a man of the land," the senator continued. "Did you realize that?"

"It seems that I recall he was in cotton before the war," Caitlyn replied. She remembered the Throckmorton plantation and the hundreds of slaves that had once worked its fields. That was a part of Texas she had never missed.

"I never understood what it is that binds a man to a mere piece of dirt," Throckmorton went on. "It's people that interest me—the towns and the cities. That's why politics is my calling. It's people and the . . . uh . . . uh—"

"Power." Caitlyn supplied the word he stumbled to find without taking her eyes from the dew-sprinkled prairie.

"It's wasn't the word I was looking for," Throckmorton assured her, "but it is close. In politics a man has the ability to change things, make things grow. He can leave his mark."

A pleased smile uplifted the corners of Caitlyn's mouth. J.D. and she had changed things all right. This country had been wild frontier when they raised the sod hut they called their first home. And they had made things grow—a few head of wild longhorns had transformed over the years into this sprawling ranch with hundreds of head of cattle. The Circle Q was quite a mark for a man—and a woman— to make in their lifetimes.

"Mrs. Caitlyn?" Moss stood in the doorway. "There's a messenger from town here. He says he's got a telegram for you. Mornin' to you, Mr. Throckmorton."

"Telegram?" Caitlyn looked up expectantly.

"Yes'um." Moss nodded. "He said for me to tell you that it's come all the way from Presidio down on the border. And Miss Katherine herself sent it."

At the word "Presidio," Caitlyn was on her feet.

"Katherine!" Caitlyn's heart tripled its tempo as she pushed past Moss and rushed through the house to the front door.

She did not give the messenger a chance to say a word. She snatched the telegram from his hand and read every word, three times, before she looked up with tears misting her eyes. Then she read the wire once again:

> I am safe. Father wounded in the shoulder. Is
> recovering. Harlan Brewster shot in the arm.
> Also recovering. General Lee recovered. Reb
> Boggs an old cuss, as ever. Your chests under
> guard. Nothing lost. Will return home when men
> can travel. Love, Your daughter Katherine.

"Damn that girl," Caitlyn muttered. "She has a fortune down there with her and two wounded men, and she sends a message this short!"

"Ma'am?" The messenger stared at her in question.

"Is Mr. J.D. and Miss Katherine all right?" This from Moss.

"Yes . . . no . . . I can't tell!" The brevity of the telegram left her flustered. "They're alive. Other than that I can't make heads or tails of this."

"If that will be all, ma'am," the messenger said, "I'll be headin' back to town."

"Yes, that will be all," Caitlyn answered, and then immediately changed her mind. "No, that won't be all. I want to send an answer to my daughter. Can you take it into Monte Verde for me?"

"No problem," the messenger answered as he reached into a back pocket and pulled forth a wrinkled pad of paper. "I even have paper and pencil to write it with."

"I want this sent to Katherine McQuay in Presidio: *On my way. Love, Your mother.*" She turned to Moss. "Find Tom Gorman and tell him to get two buckboards and my surrey ready at once. Also, he's to select twenty of our men to ride as guards."

She ordered the twenty men because of the boxes of gold coins that would have to be brought back from the border town. Caitlyn was of no mind to leave the family fortune in a vulnerable Mexican border-town bank. And from what she could make of Katherine's telegram, J.D. was in no shape to handle the task himself.

"You goin' somewhere, Mrs. Caitlyn?" Moss looked at her with a blank expression on his face.

At the same time, the messenger tapped her on the shoulder. "I'm sorry, ma'am, but company policy is that the person sending the message has to write it down and sign at the bottom."

"Company policy? What kind of . . ." She caught herself and swallowed back the anger. Taking the pad from the young man, she began to write, while she said to Moss, "We're both going to Presidio, Moss, you and I, along with twenty of our men. Now go tell Tom Gorman to get the buckboards ready and choose the men to ride with us."

"Presidio! Why, then we must be goin' to meet Mr. J.D. and Miss Katherine." Moss grinned from ear to ear, like a child who had just been told he was going to visit his grandparents. "Yes'um. I'll find Tom and tell him all you said."

Caitlyn handed the pad back to the messenger and waved him on his way. "And, Moss, tell Tom to be ready to move out by noon."

As Moss hastened toward the barn, Caitlyn hurried back into the house. She had to pack, and supplies had to be readied. And she needed to make provisions for her guests, giving instructions to the servants as to their care during her absence.

She came to a sudden halt halfway down the entry hall. Her gaze dropped to Katherine's telegram again. Her daughter had said J.D. had been wounded in the shoulder. In spite of Katherine's assurance that he was recovering, she found herself trembling. What if J.D. was injured worse than Katherine indicated? Telling her that he had only received a shoulder wound when he was more seriously hurt would be something J.D. would do, so that she would not worry.

But she did worry, and that surprised her, and made her worry even more.

Chapter Nineteen

Reb grew silent and solemn the moment he saw the surrey turn down Presidio's main street. He glanced at Katherine and then looked back at the small army of men who rode behind Caitlyn. "I believe your momma has arrived."

Katherine laughed and shook her head when she saw the apprehension—yes, even fear—on Reb's face. His reaction was incongruous with the man of courage she knew him to be. "Reb, you old fake. You're frightened of my mother."

Reb said nothing, growing more solemn with each passing second.

"Don't you know she's nothing but a pussycat?" Katherine gave the man a nudge in the ribs and a wink.

"If you say so," Reb answered. Then he mumbled, "Never heard no mountain lion ever called a pussycat."

Katherine was not given the chance to chide the old Indian scout further. Her mother's surrey with Moss at the reins, the two buckboards, and twenty riders pulled up in front of her. Caitlyn nearly jumped from the surrey as she rushed to her daughter, greeting her with a barrage of hugs, kisses, and tears. She even had a hug and kiss on the cheek for Reb, which left him twitching and shuffling his feet in wide-eyed befuddlement.

Then her eyes caught the gaudy sign that hung from the building they stood before. Indignation tinged Caitlyn's voice as she blurted, "Cantina? Your father has put you up in a cantina? I don't understand that man! He might as well have taken rooms in a bordello!"

"Mother, there is no hotel in Presidio. This was the only place Daddy could find accommodations for all of us." Katherine made no mention of playful Rosita and Maria, whom J.D. paid daily not to practice their profession inside the cantina until the McQuay party had cleared out.

"Certainly there must be a proper boardinghouse in this town!" Caitlyn refused to be mollified. "I want to speak to that man immediately!"

"He's upstairs," Katherine said. "Doctor Ortega said that both he and Harlan are to remain in bed for at least another week. After that they can travel, but the doctor said they should rest for at least three weeks after, with no strenuous activities."

"He doesn't have to get out of bed to hear what I have to say to him!" Caitlyn pointed to the cantina door. "Take me to that man. Now!"

"Mountain lion, I told you...." Katherine heard Reb mutter as she escorted her mother upstairs.

Reaching the second floor, Katherine pointed to the four rooms. "My room is there. Yours is right next to it. Reb and Harlan are in there."

"And that is your father's room." Caitlyn walked to the remaining door, threw it open without so much as a perfunctory knock, walked inside, and slammed the door behind her. "Jonathan David McQuay, what do you mean by—"

Caitlyn stumbled over her own tongue. J.D. lowered the Ojinaga newspaper he was attempting to read and smiled up at her. "Hello, Cat. Katherine said you'd be coming down to check up on us."

Everything she had intended to say faded from her mind. He looked so pale and thin. She had been right. J.D.'s injury had been more serious than Katherine's wire had let on. "Jonathan, you look like death warmed over. And this room smells like an old dog. You need some fresh air in here."

She walked to the window and nearly tripped over General Lee, who lay curled beside J.D.'s bed.

"And you look just as beautiful as you always have." The dog wagged its tail, and J.D.'s smile widened. "Before you start tearing into me, I have a few things to say, myself." He nodded to the bedroom door. "That's quite a young woman standing out there, Cat. You did yourself proud the way you raised her. I wouldn't be alive right now if it weren't for Katherine. She holds a gun a lot like you, did you know that?"

"She should. I was the one who taught her to shoot straight." Caitlyn sank to the side of his bed, shook her head, and then tenderly cupped the side of his face in her hand. "Jonathan McQuay, you still have the most uncanny way of saying the right things at the wrong time of any man I have ever met."

J.D. took her hand in both of his and squeezed it. "Have I told you that I've missed you, Cat? If I haven't, then let me say that there hasn't been an hour gone by in five years that you haven't been in my mind."

She found herself at a loss for words again. She could only stare at J.D., melting against his chest as he drew her to him. Their lips brushed lightly, and then his mouth covered hers as his right arm slipped about her waist, holding her tightly.

It took every ounce of self-control within her to summon the strength to place her palms flat against his chest and gently push away from him.

Perplexed, J.D. stared at her. "That wasn't 'no' I felt in that kiss."

"You're an injured man," she said, struggling against the desire to return to his embrace.

"I was shot in the left shoulder, Cat. *Every* other part of my body is in perfect working order." J.D. took her hand once more and eased her toward him.

Caitlyn disentangled her fingers from his and stood. "The doctor said you were to have no strenuous activities."

He tilted his head to one side and looked up at her with a sheepish, almost boyish, smile on his face. "You got me there. What I had in mind wasn't going to take just a few minutes."

Caitlyn shook her head and walked to the door. "We'll talk later, Jonathan. Right now I've twenty men and two buckboards waiting outside to take our gold back to Monte Verde. Then I have to do a little shopping." She paused. "This establishment does have a kitchen, doesn't it?"

J.D. nodded.

"Good, because from here on out, I'll be doing the cooking," she said as she opened the door. "You'll be back on your feet in no time."

"Cat," he called to her, and then said when she turned to him, "I'm glad you're here."

She smiled and nodded as she left, thinking she, too, was glad that she had come.

J.D. slipped on his coat as he stepped from the Big House. In an hour, the sun would burn away the morning chill. But until then, the coat would keep the stiffness from his left shoulder, which had recovered from Tate Lansdale's gunshot but still remembered the wound.

He glanced down at General Lee, who sat at his feet, before his gaze slowly traced across the dew-sprinkled prairie, remembering all the times he and Caitlyn had sat and watched the morning sun ignite those droplets into blazing diamonds. These past three weeks of recuperation on the Circle Q had served to remind him how much his life was made up of simple moments like that—and how much he missed them. The trail to New Mexico ahead of him seemed doubly long knowing what he was leaving behind for the second time in his life.

He pursed his lips and shook his head. But he had to leave; there was no way around it.

A rustling movement drew his head to the right. He smiled. The flowers in Caitlyn's garden were in full bloom. Most of the plants were native to the area, small and ground hugging, but with colorful blossoms. He had gathered most of them when he used to ride the range. He could not recall the number of times a brilliant flower had caught his eye and he had forgotten the strays he was chasing to take the time to dig the plant from the ground with his knife blade, wrap the root ball in burlap moistened with water from a canteen, and bring it home to Caitlyn. Then she had worked her special kind of magic, placing the new addition in her garden and providing the loving care required to make it flourish.

Amid the bluebonnets, Mexican hats, and Indian paintbrushes clustered around the Big House grew rosebushes with blossoms of red, pink, and yellow. These, too, he had brought to Caitlyn each time he had driven a herd north to the railhead, where different flowers grew.

It was by a long hedge of rosebushes that Katherine and Harlan walked hand in hand. The smile returned to J.D.'s lips. In the month since Tate Lansdale had tried to cut him down in the streets of Presidio, he had grown close to Katherine. She was quite a young woman—the kind he would have been proud to call a friend even if blood did not join them as father and daughter.

In that same time, he had reaffirmed his first evaluation of the young man at her side. Harlan Brewster had a good head on his shoulders. He had quite a few ideas about ranching and new cattle breeds, ideas that could double the productivity of this range. Besides, J.D. was pleased, it was not the Circle Q he was interested in, but his own spread. Given a few years, Harlan's Running B just might be giving the Circle Q a run for its money.

J.D. liked that. The young man's eye was on Katherine, where it was supposed to be, and not on McQuay land. When, not if, Harlan cut a place for himself in this country, it would be on his own. That was something any man could understand and respect.

The only loser in this had been young Clay Throckmorton. Katherine had spoken to him, gently but earnestly, shortly after the return from Presidio, and he had taken the news of her interest in Harlan as manfully as he had leapt to her defense on the stagecoach—Katherine had told J.D. about that incident. The boy had grit in him, for all his city ways, and he would make out all right.

Watching Katherine and Harlan now, J.D. realized it would not be that long before he would be riding back to Monte Verde. When he did, it would be to give away a very special bride.

Even Caitlyn seemed to support wholeheartedly the love that grew each day between Katherine and Harlan. And that was no little surprise to J.D. He had expected a full-blown battle when Harlan announced his intentions to woo Cat's only child. Instead, Caitlyn had given Harlan a hug and her best wishes. J.D. had thought the young man would faint, so shocked had he been by her agreeable reaction. J.D. knew he almost had.

Glancing to the east, J.D. saw the sun sitting a hand's breadth above the distant Del Norte Mountains. Whether he wanted to admit it or not, he was woolgathering and delaying the inevitable. Las Cruces lay hundreds of miles to the west, and he was getting no closer to New Mexico by standing here.

Signaling General Lee forward, he walked down the wooden gallery that ran along the back of the Big House and quickly moved to the barn. Inside he saddled the big buckskin he had purchased upon his return north. He took with him no more than he had brought. The few supplies he would need he could buy when he reached Monte Verde.

He slipped a hackamore bridle on the gelding and led him from the stall. He then looped the braided reins over his head and grasped the saddle horn, preparing to mount.

"And just where do you think you're going?"

J.D. turned to see Katherine standing by the barn door. She walked toward him. "You appeared pleasantly occupied with a certain young man. I didn't want to disturb you."

"So you were just going to ride away?"

"That's the way of it," he admitted, his eyes shifting from her face to the open range he could see through the door.

"You weren't even going to say good-bye." Katherine stared at him in disbelief.

"I was never one for formal good-byes. You know that by now." J.D. shook his head.

"Well, Jonathan David McQuay, I am not going to let you ride away like that!"

J.D. ran a hand down his neck. Katherine sounded just like Caitlyn when she spoke his name.

"The fact of the matter is, I'm not going to let you ride off at all. This is your home. This is where you belong. I haven't found my father just to lose him again. I won't allow you to ride out the way you did last time."

He had hoped to avoid this. How did a parent explain to a child, even a child that was a grown woman, how things were between her mother and father? "Katherine, I didn't just wake up one morning five years ago and ride off for no reason. It might have seemed like that to a little girl of thirteen, but that wasn't the way of it. You have to believe me. It was something your mother and I had talked out and agreed on. You see, she and I just . . . well . . . we kind of grew apart. We didn't want the same things anymore. A man and woman can't live like that, not without being at each other's throats every waking minute. We both knew that, and we cared too much about one another to live that way."

He looked at his daughter. She heard what he said, but he could not tell if she understood. "Besides, when I left Las Cruces to come after you, I had a contract to deliver two hundred saddle-broken horses to the U.S. Army in Santa Fe by the end of July. I'm not a man to leave unfinished business."

"But you love Mother, and she loves you," Katherine protested. "I can see it every time you look at each other."

J.D. drew a deep breath. He fidgeted with the reins in one hand, his hat in the other. "Katherine, I never loved a woman before your mother—or since. The trouble is—"

"The trouble is, we're too much alike."

Katherine and J.D. looked to the front of the barn. Caitlyn stood in the doorway and then approached. "Katherine, your father and I are both too mule-headed stubborn to admit that we were wrong five years ago—that somewhere along the way, we both forgot to listen to our hearts. We started listening to other, less important things. For me it was what your father calls my 'airs.' You know what I mean—all that Austin high society and fancy living. For your father, it was this land, the struggle to make it into something more than a piece of grass and dirt. People, no matter how much love they share, do stupid things like that sometimes. We let a wedge drive between us. It's something you and Harlan should always try to avoid."

J.D. stared at her, uncertainty furrowing his brow. "Cat, are you saying what I think you're saying?"

"I'm saying what you tried to say back in Presidio, but

I was too pigheaded to hear. It's time we both stopped acting like old fools and admitted to ourselves and each other that life isn't worth living when we're apart. What's past is past, Jonathan. We're not that old. There's still plenty of time for us to change and make allowances for each other, and—"

J.D. did not need to hear any more. He swept her into his arms and covered her mouth with his. This time she came to him, her arms encircling him and holding him as tightly as he held her.

When they parted, he whispered a simple "I love you" in her ear, gave her another hasty kiss, gave Katherine a hug and a wish for good luck, and mounted the buckskin and rode from the barn. He whistled to General Lee. The dog glanced back at the two women and then trotted after J.D.

"Mother!" Shock and horror filled Katherine's eyes. "You're not going to let him leave! You can't! Not now!"

Caitlyn slipped an arm around her daughter's waist and hugged Katherine to her as they walked to the front of the barn to watch J.D. leave. "You heard him. He has two hundred horses to deliver to the army by the end of July. Your father isn't a man to leave business unfinished." She glanced at her daughter. "But don't worry, I think he knows now that he has a lot of unfinished business standing right here."

A warmth spread through Caitlyn when her eyes turned back to the man who rode away from her. That warmth suffused her cheeks with a tingling blush of pink. Desire. Gratitude. Recognition of a small miracle. She had no doubt Jonathan David McQuay would return, and when he did, her love would make certain he stayed—for the rest of their lives.

★ WAGONS WEST ★

This continuing, magnificent saga recounts the adventures of a brave band of settlers, all of different backgrounds, all sharing one dream—to find a new and better life.

☐	26822	INDEPENDENCE! #1	$4.50
☐	26162	NEBRASKA! #2	$4.50
☐	26242	WYOMING! #3	$4.50
☐	26072	OREGON! #4	$4.50
☐	26070	TEXAS! #5	$4.50
☐	26377	CALIFORNIA! #6	$4.50
☐	26546	COLORADO! #7	$4.50
☐	26069	NEVADA! #8	$4.50
☐	26163	WASHINGTON! #9	$4.50
☐	26073	MONTANA! #10	$4.50
☐	26184	DAKOTA! #11	$4.50
☐	26521	UTAH! #12	$4.50
☐	26071	IDAHO! #13	$4.50
☐	26367	MISSOURI! #14	$4.50
☐	27141	MISSISSIPPI! #15	$4.50
☐	25247	LOUISIANA! #16	$4.50
☐	25622	TENNESSEE! #17	$4.50
☐	26022	ILLINOIS! #18	$4.50
☐	26533	WISCONSIN! #19	$4.50
☐	26849	KENTUCKY! #20	$4.50
☐	27065	ARIZONA! #21	$4.50
☐	27458	NEW MEXICO! #22	$4.50
☐	27703	OKLAHOMA! #23	$4.50

- -

Bantam Books, Dept. LE, 414 East Golf Road, Des Plaines, IL 60016

Please send me the items I have checked above. I am enclosing $_____
(please add $2.00 to cover postage and handling). Send check or money
order, no cash or C.O.D.s please.

Mr/Ms _____

Address _____

City/State _____ Zip _____

Please allow four to six weeks for delivery.
Prices and availability subject to change without notice.   LE-9/89